Thérèse Desqueyroux

François Mauriac was born in Bordeaux on 11 October 1885. After the death of his father when Mauriac was eighteen months old, he and his four older siblings were brought up by their mother. He studied in Bordeaux and Paris but left university to devote himself to writing, publishing a collection of poems, *Les Mains jointes (Clasped Hands)*, in 1909. He married in 1913 and the following year was mobilized to serve in the First World War with the Auxiliary Medical Squad in Thessalonica. Following the publication of several novels and poetry collections, Mauriac's major literary breakthrough came in 1922 with a novel called *Le Baiser au lépreux (A Kiss for the Leper)*. His most famous work, *Thérèse Desqueyroux*, appeared in 1927 and has been made into a film twice: first in 1962, with Emmanuelle Riva in the lead role, and more recently in 2012, in a version starring Audrey Tautou.

In 1933 Mauriac was elected a Member of the French Academy and in 1952 he received the Nobel Prize for Literature. He died in Paris in 1970.

D1354420

FRANÇOIS MAURIAC

Thérèse Desqueyroux

Translated by GERARD HOPKINS

PENGUIN BOOKS

PENGUIN CLASSICS

Published by the Penguin Group
Penguin Books Ltd, 80 Strand, London WC2R ORL, England
Penguin Group (USA) Inc., 375 Hudson Street, New York, New York 10014, USA
Penguin Group (Canada), 90 Eglinton Avenue East, Suite 700, Toronto, Ontario, Canada M4P 2Y3
(a division of Pearson Penguin Canada Inc.)
Penguin Ireland, 25 St Stephen's Green, Dublin 2, Ireland (a division of Penguin Books Ltd)
Penguin Group (Australia), 707 Collins Street, Melbourne, Victoria 3008, Australia
(a division of Pearson Australia Group Pty Ltd)
Penguin Books India Pvt Ltd, 11 Community Centre, Panchsheel Park, New Delhi – 110 017, India
Penguin Group (NZ), 67 Apollo Drive, Rosedale, Auckland 0632, New Zealand
(a division of Pearson New Zealand Ltd)
Penguin Books (South Africa) (Pty) Ltd, Block D, Rosebank Office Park,
181 Jan Smuts Avenue, Parktown North, Gauteng 2193, South Africa

Penguin Books Ltd, Registered Offices: 80 Strand, London WC2R ORL, England

www.penguin.com

Thérèse Desqueyroux first published in France in 1927
This English translation first published in the collection *Thérèse* by Eyre and Spottiswoode 1947
Published by Penguin Books 1959
This edition published in Penguin Classics 2013
001

Translation copyright © Eyre Methuen Ltd, 1972
All rights reserved

The moral right of the author and translator has been asserted

Set in Monotype Garamond
Printed in Great Britain by Clays Ltd, St Ives plc

ISBN: 978-0-141-39405-3

www.greenpenguin.co.uk

Penguin Books is committed to a sustainable
future for our business, our readers and our planet.
This book is made from Forest Stewardship
Council™ certified paper.

ALWAYS LEARNING   **PEARSON**

Contents

THÉRÈSE DESQUEYROUX

FOREWORD

Seigneur, ayez pitié, ayez pitié des fous et des
folles! Ô Créateur! peut-il exister des
monstres aux yeux de celui-là seul qui sait
pourquoi ils existent, *comment ils se sont faits,*
et comment ils auraient pu ne pas se faire. ...

CHARLES BAUDELAIRE

MANY, *Thérèse, will say that you do not exist. But I who for so
many years have watched you closely, have sometimes stopped you
in your walks, and now lay bare your secret, I know that you do.*

*I remember, as a young man, seeing you in a stuffy Court-room, at
the mercy of lawyers whose hearts were less hard than those of the over-
dressed women on the public benches. Your small face was white, your
lips scarcely visible.*

*Later still, I came on you again in a country drawing-room, a young
and ravaged woman plagued by the attentive care of aged relatives and a
foolish husband. 'What's wrong with her?' they said; 'haven't we
given her all that a girl could want?'*

*Often, since then, seeing that rather too large hand raised to your
high and lovely brow, I have been filled with wonder: often have
watched you prisoned behind that family barrier, prowling like a she-
wolf, and caught your sad, malevolent eye fixed full upon me.*

*Many will feel surprise that I should give imagined life to a creature
more odious than any character in my other books. Why, they will ask,
have I never anything to say of those who ooze with virtue and wear
their hearts upon their sleeves? People who 'wear their hearts upon
their sleeves' have no story for me to tell, but I know the secrets of the
hearts that are deep buried in, and mingled with, the filth of flesh.*

*I could have wished, Thérèse, that sorrow might have turned your
heart to God, and have long desired to see you worthy of the name of
Saint Locusta.* But had I shown you thus redeemed there would have*

* Locusta was a notorious woman poisoner who lived in Rome during
the reign of the Emperor Nero. Monsieur Mauriac's thought is here com-
pressed and difficult. The implied argument would seem to run as follows:
Thérèse, like Locusta, was a poisoner. But great sinners may, with the gift
of Grace, become great saints. My wish was that Thérèse, by virtue of
repentance, should attain sanctity, and, had she done so, she might well
have been known as Saint Locusta. – TRANSLATOR

been no lack of readers to raise a cry of sacrilege, even though they may hold as an article of Faith the Fall and Ransom of our torn and twisted natures.

I take my leave of you upon a city's pavements, hoping, at least, that you will not for ever be utterly alone.

F. M.

I

THE barrister opened a door. Thérèse Desqueyroux, in that out-of-the-way corridor of the Court-house, felt the fog upon her face and took deep breaths of it. She was afraid lest someone might be there to meet her, and held back. A man with his coat collar turned up moved out from the shadow of a plane-tree. She recognized her father.

'Case dismissed!' called the barrister; and then, turning to her:

'You can come out: there's no one here.'

She went down the damp steps. True, the small square seemed utterly deserted. Her father did not kiss her. He did not even look at her, but addressed a question to the barrister, Duros, who answered in a low voice, as though he were afraid of being overhead. The words they spoke came to her, but not plainly.

'Tomorrow I shall be officially notified that the case has been dismissed.'

'No danger of any last-minute surprises?'

'Not the least in the world. We've got it, as they say, served up on a plate.'

'After my son-in-law's evidence it was a foregone conclusion.'

'Hardly that – one can never be quite certain.'

'Once they'd got him to admit that he never counted his drops ...'

'But in cases of this kind, you know, Larroque, the evidence of the victim ...'

Thérèse spoke in a loud voice:

'There was no victim.'

'Victim of his own carelessness, I meant, Madame.'

For a brief instant the two men looked at the young woman standing there huddled in her coat. Her pale face was quite expressionless. She asked where the carriage was. Her father had told it to wait for them on the Budos road, outside the town, so as to avoid attracting attention.

They crossed the Square. Plane leaves were sticking to the damp benches. Fortunately, at this time of the year, the days were short, and their walk to the Budos road led them through some of the least frequented streets to be found thereabouts. Thérèse was between the two men. She was a head taller than either. They continued to discuss the case as though she had not been there. But her physical presence incommoded them, and they jostled her continually. She dropped back a few paces. She took off her left-hand glove and began picking at the moss which grew between the old stones of the walls they passed. Now and then a workman came by on a bicycle or a waggon. She had to flatten herself against the wall so as not to be spattered with mud. In the dim light nobody recognized her. The smell of fog and of baking bread was not merely the ordinary evening smell of an insignificant country town, it was the sweet savour of life given back to her at long last. She closed her eyes and breathed deeply of the perfume of the sleeping earth, of the wet, green grass. She tried not to listen to the little man with the short legs who never once addressed his daughter. She might have fallen into the ditch, and neither he nor Duros would have noticed it. They were no longer afraid to raise their voices.

'Monsieur Desqueyroux's evidence was first-rate. But the prescription might have made things difficult. The point was, had it, or had it not, been forged? ... Don't forget it was Dr Pédemay who laid the charge. ...'

'But he withdrew it. ...'

'All the same, her explanation ... that story of the prescription having been given her by a stranger ...'

Less because she was tired than in order to avoid hearing all this talk with which she had been deafened for weeks past, Thérèse began to walk more and more slowly. But it was useless. She could not help hearing her father's falsetto tones.

'I kept on telling her that she must cook up something better than that. Any story, I said, would be an improvement on the one she had. ...'

All that, of course, was perfectly true, and he could claim full credit for the part he had played. But why must he still harp on the subject? What he was so fond of calling the 'family honour' was safe. By the time the elections for the Senate came round the whole business would have been forgotten.

So ran Thérèse's thoughts. All she wanted was to keep well away from the two men. But so hot was their argument that they stopped dead in the middle of the road, gesticulating.

'The best thing you can do, Larroque, is to come out into the open. Take the offensive in the Sunday edition of *Le Semeur*. Or, I'll do it for you, if you'd rather. You want a good headline – "A Scandalous Rumour" – something like that ...'

'My dear chap, what's the point? It's perfectly obvious that the whole thing's been dropped. They didn't even bother to call a handwriting expert. Much better say nothing, and let it die of inanition. There's nothing I'd like better than to hit back ... but for the family's sake we've got to hush the whole business up. ...'

They were walking more quickly now, and Thérèse did not hear Duros's answer. Once more she breathed in the damp night air like someone threatened with suffocation. Suddenly there rose before her inner eye the face of Julie Bellade, the maternal grandmother whom she had never seen: never seen even in representation, for she might have sought in vain among the family possessions of the Larroques or the Desqueyroux for a portrait, a daguerreotype, a photograph of the woman about whom she knew only that one day she had just vanished. It occurred to her that she too might have been blotted out from human memory, completely obliterated, so that her own daughter, her little Marie, might never, in days to come, have found so much as a picture of the woman who had brought her into the world. As like as not, at this very moment, the child was fast asleep in her room at Argelouse, the house which she would reach late that night. There, in the darkness, the young mother would hear the even breathing of her slumbering child, would lean above the bed and drink down, like a draught of cool, refreshing water, the small sleeping life.

A barouche with its hood closed was standing drawn in to the edge of the ditch. The flanks of the two horses showed skinny in the lamplight. Beyond, to right and left, a wall of forest trees shut in the road. The summits of the nearer pines met above the twin strips of grassy verge, and beneath the arch thus formed the highway drove mysteriously on. Amid the tangle of high branches the sky had cleared for itself a twig-encumbered couch. The coachman stared at Thérèse with an expression of greedy curiosity. When she asked him whether they would get to Nizan station in time to catch the last train, he reassured her, but added that they had better get going.

'It's the last time I shall put you to all this trouble, Gardère.'

'They've finished with you, then, ma'am?'

She nodded her head. The man's eyes were still devouring her. Must she be stared at like this all the rest of her life?

'You must be very pleased, ma'am?'

Her father seemed, at long last, to have become aware of her presence. She took a hurried glance at his grubby, bilious face, at the stiff little yellowish-white bristles that covered his cheeks and stood out startlingly in the lamplight. She said in a low voice: 'I've been through so much. ... I'm at the end of my tether ...' then stopped. What was the use of talking? He wasn't listening, wasn't even looking at her. Much *he* cared about what she might be feeling. The only thing that mattered to him was his progress along the road that was to lead eventually to the Senate. Because of *her* he had met with a check, had seen his chance imperilled (all women are either fools or hysterical). Luckily, her name was no longer Larroque. She was a Desqueyroux now. At least she wouldn't have to face the Assizes. Thinking of that, he breathed more freely. His enemies, of course, would do their best to keep the wound from healing. What steps could he take about that? He must have a word with the Prefect tomorrow. It was fortunate that he'd got such a hold on the editor of *La Lande Conservatrice* ... the man had been playing about with girls once too often. ...

He took Thérèse by the arm: 'In with you, now: we mustn't dawdle.'

The barrister, in response, perhaps, to the sudden promptings of malice, or perhaps simply because he did not want to see her go off without his having exchanged a word with her, chose this moment to ask whether she would be seeing Monsieur Bernard Desqueyroux that evening.

'Naturally,' she said – 'my husband is expecting me.'

As she uttered the words she realized for the first time since leaving the Court that in a few hours from now she would be actually entering the room where her husband lay, still far from well: that there was an indefinite vista of days opening before her, and of nights that she must spend with him for ever at her side.

Since the trial began she had been living with her father on the outskirts of the little town. More than once she had made the same trip as that on which she was now embarked. But on previous occasions she had been concerned only to give her husband precise instructions, only to understand exactly what it was that Duros was saying, as she got into the carriage, about the answers that Monsieur Desqueyroux must have ready when next he was called to give evidence. She had felt no pain, no sense of embarrassment at the thought of seeing the sick man. What then had been at issue between them was not what had happened in the past, but only what should now be said or left unsaid. This need for concocting a defence had brought husband and wife closer together than they had ever been before. They were of one flesh – the flesh of their little daughter Marie. Over and over again they had rehearsed together the story they had built up for the Judge's benefit. It was simple, well-knit, proof against all subtle attacks of logic. It had been the same carriage then as now. But how impatient she had been on those occasions, how eager to finish a journey which now she wished would go on for ever! Hardly she remembered, had she taken her seat than she had longed to be already in that room at Argelouse. Again and again she would go over in her mind the instructions for which Bernard was waiting (how, for instance, he was not to be nervous about admitting that she had told him one evening of the stranger who had asked her to get a prescription made up for him, giving as an excuse the explanation that he owed the chemist money, and dared not go himself ... though Duros had been of the opinion that he had better not go so far as to say that he had blamed his wife for being imprudent). ...

But what would there be to talk about now that the nightmare was over? She could see in imagination the house in which he lay waiting – a lost and hidden place buried in a wild countryside. She had a vision of the bed standing in the middle of the stone-flagged room, of the lamp burning low amid the litter of newspapers and medicine-bottles on the table. The watchdogs, roused by the sound of the carriage, would bark awhile and then fall silent. ... All round them would be the solemn country stillness, as on those other nights when she had sat there gazing at Bernard as he struggled with his spasms of nausea. She forced herself to contemplate the immediate future, the way in which they would look at one another when they met – and then the prospect of the night ahead, the morrow, and all the days and weeks which lay before them in that house at Argelouse, with the need removed to build up a plausible version of the drama of their lives. Between them, from now on, would lie not fiction but reality. ... She was seized with sudden panic. Her face turned to the lawyer; but, addressing her words to the older man, she began to stammer:

'I expect to spend a few days with my husband, after which, if the improvement in his health is maintained, I shall come back here to my father. ...'

'You'll do nothing of the sort, my girl!' Gardère began to fidget on his box, and Monsieur Larroque lowered his voice:

'Have you completely taken leave of your senses? Abandon your husband at a moment like this? You've got to stick together from now on, till death do you part. ...'

'You're perfectly right, Papa – I don't know what I could have been thinking of to talk like that. You'll come to Argelouse, then, I take it?'

'I shall expect you as usual, Thérèse, on market days. You

will come and see me then, as you always have done in the past.'

It was extraordinary that she could not see how the least breach in the accustomed routine would blow everything sky-high. It must be clearly understood. He trusted that he could rely upon her. She had brought enough trouble on the family already. ...

'You will obey your husband. That is the best advice I can give you.'

And with these words he pushed her into the carriage.

Thérèse saw the lawyer's hand, with its coarse black nails, extended towards her.

'All's well that ends well,' he said: and he meant it. If the trial had been carried to a higher Court it would have done *him* no good. The family would have briefed Maître Peyrecave of the Bordeaux Bar. Yes, all's well ...

2

Thérèse dearly loved the musty smell of worn leather in old carriages. ... She had forgotten her cigarettes, but found comfort in the knowledge that she never enjoyed smoking in the dark. The lamps revealed the grassy verges of the road, a fringe of bracken, the bottom part of the trunks of monster pines. Heaps of stones broke the shadow of the moving vehicle. Sometimes a country waggon passed, the mules automatically keeping to the right without any movement of their dozing driver. It seemed to her that she would never get to Argelouse. She hoped that she would not. More than an hour's drive to Nizan station, then the little local train with its endless stops at every intermediate Halt. Even when they got to Saint-Clair there would be six more miles to cover in the trap (the road was so bad that no car would face it in the darkness) before Argelouse was reached. At any or all of these stages on her journey destiny might intervene to save her. The day before the verdict was to be given she had been obsessed by the thought of what would happen should the case go against her, had felt as one alert to an impending earthquake; and now she let her mind play about the self-same fantasy. She took off her hat, let her small, pale head bump against the smelly leather cushion, and surrendered her body to their jolting progress. Until this evening she had been living the life of a hunted creature. Now that her safety was assured she realized the degree of her exhaustion. With her hollow cheeks and prominent cheek-bones, with her lips parted as though for breath, and her high, magnificent forehead, she looked like a woman condemned – even though her fellow-men had found her guiltless – condemned to an eternity of loneliness. Her charm – so the world had said once – was irresistible. Yet it was no more than all possess whose faces would betray a secret torment, the throbbing of an inner wound, did they not wear themselves out in a constant effort to deceive. Deep in the recesses of this bumping carriage, moving along a road sliced through the dense darkness of the pines, sat a young woman, all defences down, gently stroking with her right hand her scorched and scalded face. Bernard's lying evidence had saved her. What would be his first words to her now? Tonight, naturally, he would ask no questions ... but tomorrow? Thérèse closed her eyes, then opened them again as the horses slowed to a walk. She tried to recognize this lift in the road. Much better not try to anticipate events, and easier, perhaps, than she had thought. Let the future look after itself. Sleep. ... Why was she no longer in the carriage? Who was that man seated at a green-baize desk? ... The examining magistrate ... that ever recurring face. ... He knew well enough that the whole defence was a put-up affair. His head moved from right to left. She was not to be discharged after all. A new fact had come to light. A new fact? She turned away lest the enemy see her ravaged countenance. 'Cast your mind back, Madame. You mentioned an old cape which you never use except when you go duck-shooting in October. Are you sure there was nothing in the inside pocket? – nothing you had forgotten? Nothing you had concealed?' Useless to protest her innocence. She felt as though she were suffocating. Without, for a single moment, taking his eyes from his prey, the magistrate laid upon the desk a tiny package closed with a red seal. In harsh, incisive tones he began to read the formula written on the label. She knew it already by heart:

Chloroform	..	..	..	..	30 grams
Aconite drops	..	..	..	..	20
Digitalin sol.	..	..	..	..	20 grams

The magistrate burst into a cackle of laughter ... the brake began to grate against the wheel: Thérèse woke up. Her lungs drew in great gulps of the misty air (they must be on the slope leading down to the stream). She used to have just such dreams when she was a girl, only then they had been about some mistake she had made in her examination, a mistake which meant that she would have to take School Certificate all over again. Tonight she felt the same relief from oppression as when, long years ago, she had woken from that particular nightmare, though she was conscious still of a faint uneasiness at the thought that her discharge had not yet been given its official form. 'Don't be silly. You know perfectly well that it will have to be notified first to your Counsel. ...'

Free ... what more could she want? It would be mere child's play to reach a *modus vivendi* with Bernard. She must be absolutely frank with him. Nothing must be left unsaid: that way, and that way only, lay salvation. All that was hidden must be brought into the light of day – and at once, tonight. Having made up her mind on this point, she was conscious of a flood of happiness. There would be time, before they reached Argelouse, for her to 'prepare her confession', as her pious friend Anne de la Trave used to say each Saturday at the time when they spent such happy holidays together. Little sister Anne, dear innocent, what an important part yours is in all this story! The really pure in heart know nothing of what goes on around them each day, each night; never realize what poisonous weeds spring up beneath their childish feet.

The dear little thing had been right when she said to Thérèse – at that time a mocking, argumentative schoolgirl: 'You've no idea how *light* one feels after telling everything and getting absolution – how lovely it is to know that the past has been wiped out, and that one can begin all over again with a clean slate.' Merely to have decided to make a clean breast of everything was enough now to give Thérèse a sense of bonds relaxed. It was a delicious sensation. 'Bernard shall know all: I'll tell him.'

What should she tell him? What should be her first confession? Could mere words ever make comprehensible that confused, inevitable conglomeration of desires, determinations, and actions unforeseen? How do those act who *know* the crimes they are committing? ... 'I *didn't* know. I never wanted to do that with which I am charged. I don't know what I *did* want. I never had the slightest idea to what that frantic urge inside me, yet outside too, was working, what destruction it would sow in its frantic progress. No one was more terrified of it than I was. ...'

A smoky paraffin lamp cast a light on the roughcast wall of the station at Nizan, and on the stationary cab. (How quickly the darkness flowed back and filled the world beyond the range of its beams!)

From a train standing at the platform came the melancholy sound of lowing, bleating animals. Gardère took Thérèse's bag and, once again, his eyes ate up her face. His wife must have given him a strict injunction to see 'how she takes it, and what she looks like'. ... Instinctively, Thérèse produced for Monsieur Larroque's coachman that famous smile of hers which led people to say: 'It never occurs to one to consider whether she's pretty or ugly. One just surrenders to her charm.' She asked him to take a ticket for her, because she felt nervous about walking through the waiting-room where two farmers' wives were seated, their baskets on their knees, their heads nodding, busy with their knitting. When he brought the ticket back she told him he could keep the change. He touched his hat, and then, gathering up the reins, turned for one last stare at his master's daughter.

The train was not yet made up. In the old days, Thérèse Larroque and Anne de la Trave, going off for the holidays, or returning at the beginning of term, had always thoroughly enjoyed this stop at Nizan. They used to eat fried eggs and bacon at the inn, and then, their arms round one another's waist, walk along the road which tonight looked so dark and threatening, though in that long dead time it had always, in Thérèse's memory, been white beneath the moon. They had laughed to see the mingling of their long black shadows, and talked, no doubt, the while about their schools, their friends, their mistresses – the one all eagerness in defence of her Convent, the other of her College. ... 'Anne!' Thérèse cried the name aloud into the darkness. It was of her that she must first tell Bernard ... Bernard, that most precise of men, who was never satisfied until he had labelled, ranged, and set aside each separate emotion, ignoring their gradations, the subtle nexus of their interchange. How make him see with his own eyes that world of shifting forms in which Thérèse had lived and suffered? It had got to be done somehow. The only possible way would be to go straight to his room, to sit down on his bed, to lead him gently on from stage to stage, until at last she reached the point at which he would stop her with a '*Now I* understand. Get up: you are forgiven.'

She tiptoed across the station-master's garden, smelling the chrysanthemums although she could not see them. There was no one in the first-class compartment which she entered, and, in any case, the light from the lamp would have been too dim to show her face. Impossible to read. But compared with her own terrible existence all inventions of the novelist would have seemed thin and colourless. She might die of shame, of anguish, of remorse, of weariness but certainly she would not die of boredom. She withdrew into one corner of the carriage and closed her eyes. Surely a woman of her intelligence must be able to make the drama of her life intelligible to another? Of course she could. Once let her pursue her confession to its end, and Bernard would raise her to her feet and say: 'Let it be, Thérèse; leave worrying now. In this house of Argelouse we will wait for death together, without trying to unravel what is over and done. I am thirsty. Please go down to the kitchen and make me some orangeade – with your own hands. I will drink it at a draught, no matter how thick it may look. What matter if its taste remind me of that morning cup of chocolate? Do you remember how sick I was, beloved? Your dear hand held my head. When I brought up all that green vomit, you did not turn away your eyes. My retchings did not frighten you. Yet how pale you looked that night when my legs went dead and lost all feeling. I shivered, do you remember? – and how staggered that fool Dr Pédemay was when he found my temperature so low, my pulse so irregular. ...'

'Ah!' thought Thérèse: 'he won't have understood. I shall have to begin again from the beginning ...' But what is the beginning where our actions are concerned? Our destiny, once we begin to try to isolate it, is like those plants which we can never dig up with all their roots intact. Would she find it necessary to go back to her childhood? But even our childhood is, in a sense, an end, a completion.

Thérèse's childhood. However sullied the stream, there is snow at its source. At school she had seemed withdrawn, a stranger to the trivial tragedies which played such havoc with her friends. The mistresses often held her up as an example. 'Thérèse asks no reward other than the joy which comes of knowing that one has achieved superior virtue. Her conscience is the light by which she lives, and it is enough. Her pride in belonging to an élite has more power to control her conduct than any fear of punishment. ...' In some such words had one of her teachers expressed herself. But Thérèse wondered, now: 'Was I really so happy, so innocent of guile? Everything which dates from before my marriage I see now as bathed in a light of purity – doubtless because that time stands out in such vivid contrast to the indelible filth of my wedded life. Looked at from the point where I now stand as wife and mother, College has all the glamour of a paradise. But at the time I did not see it so. How could I possibly have known that during those years before life had properly begun for me I was, in fact, living my true life? Pure? – Yes, I certainly was that; an angel? – perhaps, but an angel torn by passions. No matter what my mistresses might say, I suffered and made others suffer too. I delighted in the pain I caused – and knew at the hands of my friends. What then I experienced was undiluted suffering, unsoftened by remorse. Joys and agonies came to me from even the most innocent of pleasures.'

Her reward had been, when the dog days came, to feel herself worthy of Anne with whom she walked beneath the oaks at Argelouse. She had felt she must be able to say to the young pupil of the Sacred Heart: 'I can be as pure as you without all those good-conduct ribbons and all the hackneyed vocabulary of virtue. ...' Anne de la Trave was pure mainly because she was ignorant. The Ladies of the Sacred Heart hung a thousand veils between their little charges and reality. Thérèse despised them for confounding virtue with ignorance. 'You know nothing of life, darling ...' she had been wont to say in those summer days at Argelouse so long ago.

Such lovely summer days! ... Seated in the little train which now at last had started to move, she admitted to herself that she must go back in thought to them, if she was ever to see clearly what had happened. It might be incredible, but it was true, all the same, that the storms of life were already gathering above the innocent beauty of those dawn days. The morning air, too limpid and too blue – bad omen for the afternoon and evening, a warning of ravaged garden beds, of branches torn and broken of mud and filth. Never at any moment of her life had she planned her road or looked ahead. Not once had she made a sudden change of direction. The slow descent had been barely noticeable: only gradually had the pace increased. The lost woman that now she was could be seen as no different from the radiant girl who had lived those happy summers in that very Argelouse to which, at the end of all, she was creeping back, glad of the dark, concealing night.

What weariness! Could there be any point in searching out the secret springs of actions now fulfilled? Through the glass of the window she could see nothing but the reflection of her lifeless face. The rhythm of the wheels checked suddenly: there was a prolonged whistle from the engine as it nosed its way with care into a station. A lantern dangling from an outstretched arm, thick local voices, the squeal of young pigs being unloaded. Uzeste already! One more station, and they would be at Saint-Clair, and then there would be nothing between her and Argelouse but the last stage in the trap. How little time Thérèse had left in which to prepare her defence!

3

ARGELOUSE is, quite literally, a 'land's end', a place beyond which it is impossible to go, the sort of settlement which, in this part of the world, is called a 'holding' – just a few farm-steads, without church, administrative centre, or graveyard, scattered loosely round an acre or so of rye, and joined by a single ill-kept road to the market-town of Saint-Clair, six miles away. This road, with its ruts and potholes, peters out beyond Argelouse into a number of sandy tracks. From there, right on to the coast, is nothing but marshland – fifty miles of it – brackish ponds, sickly pines, and stretches of heath where the sheep, at the winter's end, are the colour of dead ash. The best families of Saint-Clair derived originally from this remote and arid corner. Towards the middle of the last century, when the grandfathers of men now living started to draw a certain amount of revenue from timber and resin as well as from livestock, the families began to establish themselves in Saint-Clair, leaving their mansion-houses at Argelouse to deterior-ate into working farms. Carved beam-ends and an occasional marble chimney-piece bear witness to an ancient splendour. Each year the buildings sag more and more beneath their weight, and here and there can be seen one of the great roofs drooping like the huge wing of an exhausted bird until it looks almost as though it were resting on the ground.

But two of these decaying dwellings still house gentlefolk. The Larroques and the Desqueyroux have left their homes at Argelouse much as they took them over from their ancestors. Jérôme Larroque, Mayor and member of the Town Council of B—, close to which stands the house where he mostly lives, would never consent to change anything on the Argelouse

24

property which he inherited from his wife (who died in child-bed while Thérèse was still a baby). It did not in the least surprise him that she should elect, as she grew older, to spend her holidays there. Each summer, at the beginning of July, she went to live in the house watched over by her father's eldest sister, Aunt Clara, a deaf old spinster who loved the solitude of this remote corner of the earth because, as she said, she was spared the sight of other people's lips silently moving, and knew that there was nothing to be heard but the sound of the wind in the pines. Monsieur Larroque was delighted to think that, in this way, he not only got rid of his daughter, but threw her into the company of Bernard Desqueyroux, whom, it had been arranged, she should some day marry, though as yet there had been no official betrothal.

Bernard Desqueyroux had inherited at Argelouse, from his father, a house which stood at no great distance from that of the Larroques. He never went there before the beginning of the shooting season, taking up residence only in October, when his whole occupation was stalking duck. In the winter this solid, level-headed young man went to Paris to pursue his law studies. In the summer he gave the minimum of time possible to his family. Victor de la Trave, whom his mother had taken as her second husband, got badly on his nerves. The man had not had 'a shilling to bless himself with', and his extravagances were the talk of Saint-Clair. Bernard found his half-sister, Anne, too young to be interesting, and it is doubtful whether he paid very much more attention to Thérèse. The neighbours looked on their marriage as a foregone con-clusion, because the two properties seemed made for fusion, and on this point the extremely commonsensical young man was of one mind with the neighbours. But he left nothing to chance and took considerable pride in the neat planning of his life. 'No one's unhappy unless he deserves to be ...' was a phrase constantly on the lips of this rather flabby youth. Up till the time of his marriage he divided his existence equally between work and pleasure. He enjoyed food, drink, and, especially, shooting, but he also, in his mother's words, 'worked like a slave'. For it was the duty of a husband to be better educated than his wife, and Thérèse had the reputation, even at an early age, of being remarkably intelligent. The general view was that she was an emancipated young woman. But Bernard knew how women can be brought to heel, and it would be no bad thing, as his mother constantly reminded him, 'to have a foot in both camps'. Old Larroque might be very useful to him. At twenty-six Bernard Desqueyroux, after travelling extensively, and with much preliminary planning, in Italy, Spain, and the Low Countries would marry the richest and the most intelligent, if not the prettiest, girl in the district: 'It never occurs to one to think whether she is pretty or ugly. One just surrenders to her charm.'

Thérèse smiled to herself as she conjured up this caricature of Bernard. 'If it comes to that, he was a good deal more refined than many of the young men I might have married.' The women of that part of France are markedly superior to the men, who, from their schooldays onwards, live in an almost exclusively male society, and never cultivate their minds. The heathland has their hearts, and their imaginations never range beyond it. They have no thought for anything but the pleasures it can give. It would, they feel, be a base betrayal on their parts to be different from the men who work their land, to speak anything but the local patois, or abandon the crude, rough manners of their neighbours. But beneath Bernard's coarse exterior there was, perhaps, something of a natural kindliness. When he was on his death-bed his tenant-farmers said: 'There won't be no more gentlemen hereabouts when he's gone.' Yes, kindliness and a certain fairness of mind – more than his share of good faith. He rarely spoke of what he did not know: he accepted his own limitations. As a young man he was not bad looking, and gave the impression of a sort of ill-conditioned Hippolytus who was less interested in young women than in the hares he coursed upon the heath. ...

But Thérèse, sitting there with her eyes closed and her face pressed against the carriage window, was conjuring up a past in which he scarcely figured. It was not the young man to whom she was engaged but who meant so little to her that now she saw in imagination bicycling through those mornings of the long ago upon the road that led from Saint-Clair to Argelouse, about nine o'clock, before the heat of the day had grown intolerable: not him, but his sister Anne. She had a vision of the girl with her face aglow, while all around the cicadas were kindling into little flickers of flame on each successive pine, and the great furnace of the heath was beginning to roar beneath the sky. Millions of flies rose in a cloud above the blazing ling. 'Put on your coat before you come indoors; it's like an ice-house ...' Aunt Clara would say, adding, 'Wait till you've cooled down before you have a drink.' To the deaf old lady Anne shouted useless words of greeting: 'Don't yell yourself hoarse, darling; she can understand all you say by lip-reading. ...' But in vain would the young girl try to articulate each word, twisting her tiny mouth into the most agonizing grimaces. The aunt merely guessed and answered at random, so that the two friends had to take refuge in flight so as to be free to laugh in privacy.

From the darkness of the railway carriage she gazed at that unsullied season of her past – unsullied, but lit by a vague and flickering happiness. Fitful and unsure that happy time had been, while as yet she knew nothing of the part she would be called upon to play upon the world's stage. As she sat with Anne on a red rep sofa with a photograph album propped against her knees, no hint had come to warn her that the portion reserved for her in life's lottery would be a darkened drawing-room set in the merciless glare of summer heat. Whence had come all that happiness? Anne did not share a single one of Thérèse's preferences. She hated reading, loved only sewing, chattering, and laughing. She had not one idea in her head, while Thérèse devoured with indiscriminate avidity the novels of Paul de Kock, the *Causeries de Lundi*, *L'Histoire du Consulat*, and anything else that she could find lying about in the cupboards of an old country house. They had not a taste in common except that of being together through those afternoons when the blazing sky laid siege to human beings barricaded in the half-light of their shrouded rooms. Now and again Anne would get up and go to see whether the heat had abated. But through the half-opened shutters the blinding glare would pounce like a great stream of molten metal, till it almost burned the carpet, and all must be again shut tight while human beings went once more to earth.

Even at dusk, when the sun had come so near its setting that only the very lowest sections of the pine trunks were reddened with its light, and a belated cicada was still scraping away for dear life almost at ground-level, there was still an airless heat beneath the oaks. The two girls would lie at full length on the ground as though on the shores of a lake. Great storm clouds hinted at shapes which formed only to change almost at once and vanish. No sooner had Thérèse caught a glimpse of the winged woman whom Anne had seen pictured in the sky than she was gone again, and nothing was left but what the younger girl described as 'a funny sort of sprawling animal'.

When September came they could venture out after luncheon and wander through the parched land. No tiniest stream of water flowed at Argelouse. Only by walking a long way over the sandy heath could they hope to reach the head-waters of the rivulet which went by the name of La Hure. It carved a myriad courses through low-lying meadows laced with alder-roots. Their feet turned numb in the ice-cold current, and then, no sooner dry, were burning hot again. They would seek the shelter of one of the huts set up in October for the guns who went out after duck. It served them as the shuttered drawing-room had done earlier in the year. They had nothing to say to one another. No word passed. The minutes flew as they lay there innocently resting. They were as still and motionless as the sportsman who, spying a flight of birds, imposes silence with a movement of the hand. To have stirred so much as a finger, so it seemed to them, would have set scurrying in fright their chaste, their formless happiness. It was Anne, always, who moved first – eager to be at the business of killing larks at sundown, and Thérèse, though she hated the sport, would follow, so hungry was she for the other's company. In the hall Anne would take down the rook-rifle which fired so light a charge that there was no recoil. Her friend, standing on a bank, would watch her in the field of rye, aiming at the sun as though in readiness to shoot it from the sky. At such moments she had always put her fingers in her ears. High in the blue, the bird's shrill song of rapture broke and dropped to silence, and the girl with the gun would pick up the wounded body, tenderly pressing it in her hand, kissing the still warm feathers, before she strangled it.

'Coming tomorrow?'

'Oh no – not every day.'

She did not want to see her every day – a sensible resolve which called for no argument. It would have seemed pointless to Thérèse to make a protest. Anne preferred not to come. There was no particular reason why she should not, but what was the point in their seeing one another every day? If they did, she had said, they would end by getting bored. To which Thérèse replied: 'Of course we should – you mustn't make a duty of it. Come when you feel like it, when you have nothing better to do. ...' And her schoolgirl friend would bicycle away down the darkening road, ringing her bell.

Then Thérèse would go back to the house – the farm labourers greeting her from afar, the children shyly keeping their distance. It was the hour at which the sheep lay dotted in the oak-trees' shade. Suddenly at the shepherd's call, they would huddle into a group. Her aunt would be waiting for her at the front-door, talking unceasingly, as deaf folk do, to keep the girl from speaking to her. Why so restless? She had no wish to read, no wish to do anything in particular, only to resume her aimless wandering. 'Don't go far; dinner's just ready.' She would find her way back to the road – empty now as far as the eyes could reach. She would hear the gong sound from the kitchen entrance. Perhaps, this evening, they would have to light the lamp. The silence was no deeper for the deaf woman sitting motionless with her hands folded in her lap than for the girl with the faintly hollowed cheeks.

Oh, Bernard, Bernard, how shall I fit *you* into this tumbled world, you of the blind, implacable race of simple souls? 'But', thought Thérèse, 'as soon as I start speaking he will interrupt. "Why did you marry me?" he will ask. "I never ran after you." ...' Why *had* she married him? It was true that he had shown no eagerness. She remembered how his mother, Madame Victor de la Trave, used to say to anyone who would listen: 'He would have been only too ready to wait, it was she who made the running – she, she, she! Her code is different from ours. She smokes, for instance, like a chimney. It is a sort of pose. But she's sound at heart, as good as gold. We'll soon teach her sense. ... We're not altogether happy about the marriage. ... Oh yes ... I know all about the Bellade grandmother ... but that's all over and done with. There was never anything that could really be called a scandal – they hushed up everything very successfully. Do you believe in heredity? Of course, the father has the *most* undesirable ideas, but it's only fair to say that he's never set her any but the best example. He may not be religious, but, for all that, he really is a saint – and very influential. It takes all sorts to make a world, and one has to make allowances. Besides, though you might not believe it, she's richer than we are. It's hard to credit, but it is so. And she simply adores Bernard – which is no bad thing. ...'

Yes, it was true she had adored him. Her feeling had been perfectly natural, and there had been no need for her to put constraint upon herself. Each time she looked at him in the drawing-room at Argelouse, or beneath the trees at the far end of the field, her eyes had been eloquent of simple love. So easy a conquest had flattered the young man, though it would be scarcely true to say that it surprised him. 'Don't play with her feelings,' his mother had kept on saying: 'she's eating her heart out for you.'

'I married him because ...' Frowning in deep thought, one hand shielding her eyes. Thérèse tried to remember.

There had, of course, been the childish delight with which she had looked forward to becoming Anne's sister-in-law as a result of that marriage, though it had been Anne, really, who had found the prospect so peculiarly 'amusing'. To

Thérèse it did not mean a great deal. The acres which Bernard stood to inherit had not left her indifferent – why should she be ashamed to admit it? She had always had 'the sense of property in her blood'. Often when, at the end of interminable meals, the cloth had been removed, and the drinks began to circulate, she had stayed behind with the men, held there by the talk of farm matters and pit-props, of mineral deposits and turpentine. She took a passionate delight in estimating the value of land. There could be little doubt that the idea of controlling so great a stretch of forest territory had exercised over her an irresistible fascination. 'He, too, was in love with my trees. ...' Perhaps, though, she had yielded to a deeper and less obvious feeling which now she was striving to set in the clear light of day; had hoped to find in marriage not pride of possession and the opportunity to dominate so much as a refuge. Might it not be argued that what had precipitated her into Bernard's arms had been, in some sort, a movement of panic? As a child she had been eminently practical, instructed in economies and household management. She was eager to assume her rightful position, to occupy the place that she was destined to fill. She wanted to be re-assured, to feel that she was protected against some danger the precise nature of which she did not understand. Never had she seemed so sensible as during the months of her engagement. She embedded herself in the substance of her new family, made it her object to 'settle down'. She had entered, as it were, into an Order. She had sought safety, and found it.

She remembered how, during the spring which preceded their marriage, they had once walked together down the sandy track which led from Argelouse to Vilméja. The shrivelled oak-leaves were still showing as dirty patches against the blue. The dried tangle of last year's bracken was thick upon the ground, the tender stalks of new growth striking a note of bright and acid green. Bernard said: 'Be careful of your cigarette. Even at this time of year it might start a fire. The heath is already without water.'

'Is it true,' she asked, 'that you can get prussic acid from bracken?' Bernard did not know whether it would be enough to provide a potent dose of poison. With tender concern he had questioned her on the subject. 'Are you so anxious to die?' At that she laughed, and he had said that really she was becoming more like a child every day. She remembered how she had closed her eyes, while he took her little head between his great hands and whispered in her ear: 'There's still a lot of foolishness in there.' And she had replied: 'Then, Bernard, it's for you to get rid of it.' They had watched the bricklayers at work adding a room to the farmhouse at Vilméja. The owners – people from Bordeaux – were planning to have the last of their sons, the one who 'suffered with his chest', live there. His sister had died of the same complaint. Azévédo was their name, and Bernard expressed considerable contempt for them. 'They swear by all that's holy that they've got no Jewish blood, but just look at them – and consumptive into the bargain. They seem to be generously afflicted with every ailment.'

Thérèse, at that time, was in a placid state of mind. Anne was coming home from her Convent at Saint-Sebastian for the wedding. She would pair off with the Deguilheim boy as best man. She had asked Thérèse to describe, 'by return of post,' what the other bridesmaids were going to wear. Couldn't she get her a few cuttings of the material? It would be better all round if they chose colours that would go together. ... Never had Thérèse known such peace – or what seemed to her like peace, though it was but a half-sleep, the torpor of the snake within her breast.

4

THE day of their wedding had been stiflingly hot. In the poky little church of Saint-Clair the women's chatter had drowned the wheezy harmonium, and the incense had waged a losing battle with the smell of human bodies. It was then that the sense of being utterly abandoned had come over Thérèse. She had entered this cage like a sleep-walker, to wake with a feeling of miserable and defenceless youth at the sound of the heavy gate clanging to behind her. Nothing had changed, but she felt somehow that the feeling of abandonment involved more people than herself alone. She was fated to smoulder there, deep in the very substance of this family, like a damped-down fire worming its way beneath the heather, getting a hold first on one pine-tree, then on another, till finally the whole forest would blaze like a wilderness of torches. In all that crowd there was no face save Anne's on which her eyes could rest with a sense of finding peace. But the childish happiness of the younger girl kept her isolated from Thérèse. Oh, that happiness! It was as though she had no realization that they were to be separated that very evening, not only in space, but by reason of what Thérèse was about to suffer – of that irremediable outrage to which her innocent body would have to submit. Anne would remain upon the bank among the still untouched. Thérèse, very soon, would be one of the herd of those who have served their purpose. She remembered how, in the vestry, she had bent to kiss the laughing little face lifted to her own, and how she had realized suddenly the nothingness of everything round which she had built a universe of vague joys and sorrows no less vague. In the space of a few seconds she had seen the infinite disproportion between the mysterious promptings of her heart and the charming young countenance with its blotches of powder.

Long afterwards, at Saint-Clair and at B—, people talking of the wedding at Gamache (where more than a hundred tenant-farmers had eaten and drunk beneath the oaks) recalled that the bride – 'who isn't what you'd call really pretty, though she's the very embodiment of charm' – had looked quite ugly, almost hideous – 'so unlike herself, as though she had been somebody quite different. ...' What they meant was that her appearance had not been as it usually was. They blamed her white dress, the heat. Her real face they did not see.

When evening put an end to this half countryfied, half middle-class wedding, the car in which the newly married couple were driving away was forced to slow down because of the cheering crowd of guests, bright with the dresses of the girls. On the road, littered with acacia blooms, they passed zigzagging waggons driven by oafs who had drunk too much. Thérèse, brooding on the night that had followed, murmured, 'It was horrible! ...' then checked herself: 'No, it wasn't, not so horrible as all that. ...' Had she truly suffered on their trip to the Italian Lakes? No. She had been playing a desperate game, had been intent only on not giving herself away. A young man engaged can easily be taken in: not so a husband. No matter what lies the tongue may utter, the dissimulations of the body demand a different skill. Not everyone can ape desire and joy and happy languor. Thérèse learned how to accommodate her flesh to these new deceptions, and found a bitter pleasure in the task. Helped by her imagination, she made herself believe that for her too there might be pleasure of a sort within that world of the senses across whose threshold she had, under a man's compulsion, stepped. Of a sort, but of what sort? Much as when looking at a landscape shrouded in mist we fancy what it must be like in sunshine, so did Thérèse contemplate the delights of the flesh.

How easy it had been to take Bernard in! – Bernard of the vacant gaze, Bernard for ever worried lest the numbers on the pictures did not correspond with those in his Baedeker; satisfied if he could see, in the shortest possible time, all that there was to be seen. He remained imprisoned in his own pleasure like one of those charming little pigs whom it is so amusing to watch through the railings rooting about delightedly in their stye. ('And I was the stye,' thought Thérèse.) He always looked so much in a hurry, so busy, so serious. He was a man of method. 'Do you think it's altogether wise?' Thérèse would sometimes ask, appalled by the extent of his virility. Laughingly he reassured her. Where had he learned to draw such fine shades of discrimination in all matters pertaining to the flesh, to distinguish between what a decent man may or may not permit himself in the matter of sadistic self-indulgence? He was never for a moment in doubt. Once, when they stopped for a night in Paris on their way back, he pointedly left a music-hall where the performance

34

had shocked him. 'To think that *foreigners* should see that! It's a disgrace. That's the sort of thing they judge us by! ...' It amazed Thérèse to think that this Puritan should be one and the same as the man whose sensual ingenuities would be forced upon her in less than an hour's time. 'Poor Bernard! – no worse than anybody else! The truth is that desire transforms a man into a monster, so that he becomes utterly unlike himself. Nothing is so severing as the frenzy that seizes upon our partner in the act. I always saw Bernard as a man who charged head-down at pleasure, while I lay like a corpse, motionless, as though fearing that, at the slightest gesture on my part, this madman, this epileptic, might strangle me. As often as not, balanced on the very edge of the ultimate excruciation, he would discover suddenly that he was alone. The gloomy battle would be broken off, and Bernard, retracing his steps, would, as it were, stand back and see me there, like a dead body thrown up on the shore, my teeth clenched, my body cold to his touch.'

There had been but one letter from Anne – who disliked writing – but, by some miracle, it contained not a single line which Thérèse could find displeasing. A letter expresses not so much what we really feel as what we know we ought to feel if it is to bring pleasure to the recipient. Anne complained that since the Azévédo's son had come to Vilméja she could no longer take her walks in that direction. She had seen, from a distance, his invalid chair standing among the bracken. She had a horror of consumptives.

Thérèse read the pages over and over again, and expected to hear no more from her friend. What, then, was her surprise, when the post arrived (on the morning following the interrupted visit to the music-hall), to see Anne de Trave's handwriting on three separate envelopes. They had been travelling fast, and the bundle of letters had followed them from one poste-restante to another, until finally it had caught up with them in Paris. They 'were in a hurry', Bernard had said, 'to get back to their nest'. The real reason was that their being together no longer gave him any happiness. He was

bored to death away from his guns, his dogs, and the inn
where the Picon grenadine had a different taste from anywhere
else. His wife was so cold, so mocking. She never showed
pleasure even if she felt any, would never talk about what
really interested him. ... As to Thérèse, she longed to be
back in Saint-Clair. She was like a transported criminal, sick
to her soul of transit prisons, and anxious only to see the
Convict Island where she would have to spend the rest of her
life.

Very carefully she deciphered the date on each of the three
envelopes, and was already opening the earliest of the series,
when Bernard uttered an exclamation. She could not hear his
words, because the window was open and the motor-buses
were changing gear at the crossing beneath. He had stopped
in the middle of shaving to read a letter from his mother.
Thérèse could still see in imagination the cellular undervest,
the strong, bare arms, the pale skin, and the sudden flood of
raw scarlet which suffused his neck and face. The July morning was already stifling. The smoke-grimed sunlight made the
dreary house-fronts beyond their balcony look dirtier even
than usual. He came close to her. 'This really is a bit much!' he
exclaimed. 'I must say, your friend, Anne's, going too far!
Who would ever have thought that my young sister ...'

Thérèse looked at him inquiringly, and he went on:

'She's gone and fallen in love with young Azévédo – have
you ever heard of such a thing? ... No, I'm not joking ...
with that wretched consumptive they've been enlarging
Vilméja for! ... Looks pretty serious, too. She says she'll wait
until she's of age. ... Mother writes that she's carrying on like
a lunatic. I only hope the Deguilheims don't get wind of it. ...
I wouldn't put it beyond young Deguilheim to sheer off altogether. Are those letters from her? ... Go on, open them ...
they may tell us something more.'

'I want to read them in their proper order. Besides, I'm not
sure that I've any right to let you see them.'

How typical of her! ... always making things more complicated. Well, all that mattered was that she should force the
girl to see sense.

'My parents rely on you. ... You've got so much influence over her ... oh yes, you have. ... They regard you as their only hope of salvation.'

While she dressed, he rushed off to send a telegram and to reserve two seats in the southern express. It was time she started packing.

'What are you waiting for? Why don't you read the letters?'

'I'm waiting until you've gone out.'

For a long time after the door had slammed behind him she lay there smoking cigarette after cigarette and staring at the dirty gold lettering on the opposite balcony. Then she opened the first of the envelopes. Surely these burning words could never have been written by the dear little simpleton, the Convent-bred child, of her memories? How could this song of songs have burst from the dry little heart she had known? – for it *was* dry, as she knew only too well ... this long, this happy wail as of a woman possessed, this cry torn from a body almost dead with joy at the first onset of love?

... When I met him, I couldn't believe it was he. He was playing with the dog, running about and shouting. How could he have been behaving so if he was a sick man? But he's not a sick man. It's only that they are being careful because of the family history. He's not even delicate – just rather thin, and used to being spoiled and cosseted. ... You wouldn't know me. I go and fetch his coat for him when it gets cool. ...

Had Bernard come back into the room at that moment he would have realized that the woman seated on the bed was not his wife at all, but someone completely unknown to him, some strange, nameless creature. She threw away her cigarette and opened the second envelope.

... I'll wait just as long as I have to. I'm not afraid of anything they can do to stop me. My love takes no account of obstacles. They are keeping me at Saint-Clair, but Argelouse is near enough for Jean and me to meet. Do you remember the duck-shooting hut? It was you, darling, who chose the very places where I was later to know supreme happiness. ... Please don't jump to conclusions

37

and start thinking that we do anything wrong. He's so fastidious! you can't have any idea what he's like. He's done a terrible lot of studying and reading, just like you, but I don't mind it in a young man, and I never feel that I want to tease him about it. What wouldn't I give to know as much as you do! You've got your happiness already, darling, and I don't know anything about it yet. But it must be very wonderful if just the promise of it can be so heavenly! When I sit with him in the little hut where you used to enjoy our picnics so much, my happiness is like something solid. I feel that I can almost touch it. But I keep on telling myself that there is a still greater happiness to come, something bigger and lovelier than this. And then, when Jean goes away looking so pale, the memory of the kisses I have had, and the thought of the ones I'm going to have next day, make me deaf to the complaints, the prayers, and the reproaches of the poor fools who don't *know* ... who never have known ... Darling, forgive me. I'm talking about this happiness of mine as though you too were one of those who don't know, whereas I'm only a novice compared with you. ... I'm quite sure that you'll take our part against the people who are making us miserable. ...

Thérèse opened the third envelope. It contained only a few scribbled words:

... Come to me, darling. They've separated us. They never let me out of their sight. They think you'll be on their side. I've said that I will abide by your judgement. ... I'll explain it all to you when we meet. He's not sick. ... I am happy and terribly unhappy at the same time. I am happy at the idea of suffering for his sake, and I adore his misery because it is a sign that he truly loves me. ...

She read no further. As she slipped the sheet back into its envelope, she noticed a photograph which at first she had not seen. Standing close to the window, she studied the pictured face. It was that of a young man whose head seemed too large because the hair was so thick. She recognized the spot where the snapshot had been taken, the bank on which Jean Azévédo was standing, looking like the young David (behind him was an open heath on which sheep were browsing). He had his coat over his arm, and his shirt was partly open. ... 'He calls it the extreme point to which we can decently allow ourselves to go. ...' Thérèse raised her eyes, and was surprised at her own appearance in the glass. Only with a great effort could she have unclenched her teeth or swallowed her saliva. She dabbed her forehead and temples with eau-de-Cologne. 'She has found the secret of happiness ... and what about me? ... Why shouldn't I find it too?' The photograph was still lying on the table. Beside it glinted a pin.

'I did it – yes, I ...' In the bumpy train which was gathering speed as it took the downward slope she said again and again to herself: '... Two years ago, in that hotel bedroom, I took the pin, and I pierced the photograph of that young man just where the heart should be – not in a fit of temper, but quite calmly, as though I were doing a perfectly ordinary thing. Then I went to the lavatory, threw the photograph with the hole in it into the pan, and pulled the plug. ...'

When Bernard came back, he was surprised to find her looking solemn – looking as though she had been thinking hard, had already decided what was best to do. But it was wrong of her to smoke so much ... she was poisoning herself. ... One shouldn't, she said, pay too much attention to the whims of a young girl. She felt sure that she could make her see sense. ... Bernard longed for reassurance. The feel of their return tickets in his coat pocket gave him a little thrill of pleasure. Especially did it flatter his pride to think that his relations should turn to his wife for counsel. He told her that, extravagance or no extravagance, they would have their last luncheon at one of the restaurants in the Bois. In the taxi he talked to her of his plans for the shooting season. He couldn't wait to try out the dog that Balion was training for him. His mother wrote that the mare had been treated with hot needles and was no longer lame. ... When they got to the restaurant they found very few people there. The long row of waiters made them feel nervous. Thérèse remembered the mingled smell of geraniums and pickles that had hung about the place. Bernard had never before tasted Rhine wine. 'It costs a pretty penny, but we don't celebrate every day.' His body hid the room from her. Beyond the great windows silent cars kept gliding up and stopping. She noticed a faint movement in the region of his ears, and knew that it came from the muscles of his scalp. After the first few glasses of wine he turned excessively red. He looked like a fine, handsome, country-bred fellow. The only thing wrong with him was that for the last few weeks he had not had enough fresh air and exercise to absorb his daily ration of food and drink. She felt no hatred of him, but simply a wild desire to be alone with her pain, to discover where it was that the blow had struck her! If only he were not with her there: if only she had not got to make such an effort to eat her lunch and smile, to compose her features and to keep her eyes from blazing. If only she could fix her mind freely upon the mysterious despair which seemed to have seized upon her. ... A fellow-creature had managed to escape from the desert island where by rights they should have been together till the end, had crossed the chasm which kept her from the rest of the world, and gone back to it – had moved from one universe to another. ... No, it wasn't that. No one ever goes from one universe to another. Anne had always belonged to the race of simple souls who are content merely to be alive. Thérèse, looking at her in the old days of their lonely outings, lying asleep with her head against her friend's knees, had seen only a wraith. The real Anne de la Trave had been hidden from her, the girl who now ran to meet Jean Azévédo in a lonely shooting hut between Saint-Clair and Argelouse.

'What's the matter with you? You're eating nothing. Pity to leave food on your plate, considering what we're paying. Is it the heat? Not going to faint, are you? ... Can't, surely, be the first signs, already?'

She smiled, but only with her lips. She said that she was thinking about this adventure of Anne's (she had got to talk about Anne). When Bernard announced that he was perfectly easy in his mind now that she had taken the affair in hand, she asked him why his parents were so set against the marriage. He thought she was laughing at him, and begged her not to begin playing at paradoxes.

'To begin with, you know as well as I do that they're Jews. Mamma knew old Azévédo – the one who refused to be baptized.'

But Thérèse maintained that some of the oldest families in Bordeaux were Portuguese Jews.

'The Azévédos were somebody when *our* ancestors were a miserable lot of shepherds shaking with fever in the marshes.'

'Oh, for Heaven's sake, Thérèse, don't argue for the sake of arguing. Jews are Jews all the world over; besides, this particular family is thoroughly degenerate – eaten up with tuberculosis. Everyone knows that.'

The gesture with which she lit her cigarette had always shocked Bernard.

'What did your own grandfather die of, and his father? When you married me did it ever occur to you to inquire into the nature of my mother's last illness? Don't you think that we could find a sufficient number of consumptives and syphilitics in our own family tree to poison the whole world?'

'That's going beyond a joke, Thérèse, even if you are saying it only in fun and to get a rise out of me. I won't have you talking like that about the family!'

He was thoroughly annoyed and on his dignity – wanting to take a high line, yet, at the same time, anxious not to look a fool in her eyes. But she wouldn't give up her point.

'I can't help laughing when I see our precious families burrowing away in their dignity like a lot of blind moles! Their horror of the more obvious blemishes is only equalled by their indifference to those that don't happen to be generally known – and there are plenty of *them* in all conscience! Take yourself, for instance: aren't you always talking about "secret diseases", as though all mortal ailments weren't, by definition, secret? Our families never give them a thought, though they're careful enough not to wash their dirty linen in public. If it wasn't for the servants, one would never know a thing. Fortunately, there always *are* the servants. ...'

'I'm not going to discuss the matter with you. When you're in one of these moods the only thing to do is to wait until it's over. With me it doesn't matter. I realize that you say these things just to pull my leg: but they wouldn't be very well received at home. We're not in the habit of treating family matters as a joke.'

41

Always the family! Thérèse let her cigarette go out. She stared before her, seeing in imagination the cage with its innumerable bars, each of which was a living person, a cage full of eyes and ears, in which she would have to spend the whole of her life, squatting motionless, her chin on her knees, her arms clasped about her legs, waiting for death.

'Oh, don't look like that, Thérèse! If only you could see yourself! ...'

She smiled, readjusting the mask.

'It was just my fun. ... What an old silly you are, my dear!'

But when, in the taxi, Bernard crept close to her, she pushed him away, setting a distance between them.

On that last evening before their return to the country they went to bed at nine o'clock. Thérèse took something to make her sleep, but unconsciousness, too eagerly sought, evaded her. For a moment, indeed, she sank into oblivion, but Bernard, with a mutter of incomprehensible words, turned towards her, and she felt the heat of his great body against her own. She avoided him, seeking the extreme edge of the mattress in an effort to avoid the burning contact. But a few minutes later he lumbered towards her again, as though his flesh sought blindly its accustomed prey even in the insensibility of sleep. Roughly she pushed him from her once more, though without waking him. ... If only she could get free of him once and for all – could thrust him from the bed into the outer darkness!

Across the length and breadth of the shadowed city the motor horns were answering one another like the dogs and the fowls at Argelouse when the moon rose. No breath of freshness mounted from the street. She turned on the lamp, and, propped upon her elbow, gazed at the motionless male beside her – a male in his twenty-seventh year. He had thrown back the blankets; his breathing was inaudible, and the ruffled hair fell in a mass over his still unwrinkled forehead, over the as yet unscored temples. He lay sleeping there, a vulnerable and naked Adam, deep in a slumber that seemed eternal. She pulled a sheet over him, got up, found one of the letters in the middle of reading which she had been disturbed, and took it to the lamp.

... If he told me to follow him, I should leave everything, and never once turn back. We kiss, but on the verge of the ultimate surrender hold back, checked not by my resistance but by his power of restraint. It is truer to say that it is he who resists me, because I long for the extreme of passion, the mere approach of which, he says, surpasses all other pleasures. To hear him talk, one would think that last decisive step was never to be taken. He makes it a matter of pride to hold back on the precipitous slope. Once one lets oneself go, he says, it is impossible to stop. ...

She opened the window and tore the letter into tiny fragments. She hung there, leaning out over the deep gulf of stone which, in this hour before the dawn, echoed to the sound of a passing cart. The scraps of paper fluttered down to perch on the balconies of the lower floors. She caught a smell of growing things. From what countryside had it come to invade this wilderness of asphalt? She saw in imagination the stain made by her body lying crushed and mangled on the pavement – and all around a milling crowd of loiterers and policemen. ... You'll never kill yourself, Thérèse, your imagination is far too vivid! As a matter of fact, she had no wish to die. An urgent task awaited her – not of vengeance nor of hate. The little fool, far away at Saint-Clair, who was so sure that happiness was possible, must be made to see with *her* eyes, be made to understand that no such thing as happiness existed. That at least, if nothing else, they must have in common – boredom, the sense that no high destiny awaited them, or overriding duty. They must learn that there was nothing worth the winning save the squalid humdrum of the daily round – a loneliness without hope of consolation.

The first light was touching the roof-tops. She went back to the man lying there, motionless, upon the bed. But no sooner had she slipped between the sheets than he moved towards her.

When she awoke she was clear-headed and sensible. Why had she made such a to-do about what was really quite simple?

The family was calling on her for help. She would do what the family wanted. In that way only could she keep to the beaten track. When Bernard began to argue again that it would be disastrous if anything happened to prevent Anne's marriage to the Deguilheim boy, she agreed. The Deguilheims were not of their world. The grandfather might have tended sheep, but they owned the best forest land for miles around, and Anne, after all, was no heiress. All she could hope for from her father was a few acres of vineyard in the fens round Langon – and they were flooded out every other year. Nothing must be allowed to get in the way of that marriage.

The smell of chocolate made Thérèse feel sick. This vague bodily discomfort served to confirm her other symptons: she was already pregnant. 'Better get it over early,' said Bernard; 'and then one needn't bother any more about it.' He gazed with respect at the woman who bore within her the future master of unnumbered trees.

5

SAINT-CLAIR – already! Thérèse took the measure of the road her thoughts had come. Could she ever get Bernard to follow her so far? It was scarcely to be hoped that he would be willing to share her slow progress along that tortuous way. Yet, all the really important things still remained to be said. 'Even if I do manage to get him to the point which I've reached so far, what a lot will still have to be explained.' She brooded over the puzzle of her own existence. Silently she questioned the young middle-class married woman whom everyone had praised for her level-headedness when first she settled down with her husband in Saint-Clair. She revived the memory of those first weeks of the new life in the cool, dark house belonging to her parents-in-law. The shutters on the windows which looked into the Square were kept always closed, but in the left-hand wall a barred grille gave a glimpse of the garden aflame with heliotrope, geraniums, and petunias.

Between the old couple tucked away in the shadowed drawing-room on the ground-floor, and Anne wandering in the garden which she was forbidden to leave, Thérèse came and went, privy to all that was going on. To her mother-in-law she said: 'Give her her head a bit, suggest that she should travel for a while before making up her mind. I think I can promise that she'll agree: and then, while you're away, I'll act.' But how? The parents had a vague idea that she meant to scrape acquaintance with young Azévédo. 'A frontal attack won't do you any good, mother.' From Madame de la Trave she gathered that nothing definite had occurred as yet. Heaven be thanked for that! Mademoiselle Monod, the post-mistress, was the only other person in the secret. She had held up several of Anne's letters. 'But she's as secret as the grave. Besides, we've got a hold on her. *She* won't gossip!'

'We must do our best,' Victor de la Trave kept on saying, 'to spare her as much pain as possible.' In the old days he had given in to all Anne's whims, no matter how fantastic. But now he had to admit that his wife was right. 'One can't,' he said, 'make an omelet without breaking eggs'; and, 'She'll live to thank us.' Perhaps, but meanwhile, wasn't she making herself ill? Husband and wife fell silent, gazing vaguely about them. In their hearts, no doubt, they felt for the poor child drooping in the summer heat. She turned in disgust from all food. She trod the flowers underfoot without noticing them, padding up and down behind the garden railing like a bitch in heat looking for some way of escape. ... Madame de la Trave shook her head: 'I can't eat for her, can I? She stuffs herself with fruit and leaves her plate untouched at meals.' And Victor: 'She'd live to blame us if we gave our consent – if only because of the miserable, sickly brats she'd bring into the world. ...' His wife was angry because he seemed to be trying to find excuses for their attitude. 'Fortunately, the Deguilheims are not back yet. It's a good thing for us that they've set their hearts on a marriage with their son ...' Only when Thérèse had left the room did they put into words the question which was stirring in both their minds: 'What ideas can they have been stuffing her with at the Convent?

45

Here, at home, she's had nothing but good examples, and we've been so careful about the books she reads. ... Thérèse says there is nothing more calculated to turn a young girl's head than the sort of love-stories that are recommended for family reading ... but, of course, she adores being paradoxical. ... Besides, Anne has never had a passion for books, which is *such* a blessing. We've never had to pull her up on that account. In the matter of reading she's her parents' daughter all right. It probably *would* be a good thing if she could have a change of air. ... Don't you remember how quickly she picked up when we took her to Salies after she'd had the measles and a touch of bronchitis at the same time? We'd go anywhere she liked – one can't say more than that. She has, really, very little to complain about.' Monsieur de la Trave gave a low sigh. 'A trip with us? – that wouldn't do any good,' he answered. 'What's that?' inquired his wife, who was slightly deaf. What memory of some former lovers' journey had come back suddenly into the old man's mind? For so long now he had been comfortably settled into the smooth existence of every day that it seemed strange he should be moved by a recollection from the golden time of his passionate youth.

Thérèse went into the garden to talk to the young girl. Anne was wearing a last-year's frock which had now grown too large for her.

'Well?' she cried, as her friend joined her. Thérèse could see again every detail of the scene – the burned-up paths, the dry, brittle meadow-grass; could smell in memory the hot geraniums. The girl had looked, that August afternoon, as though she were more utterly consumed than any growing thing. Now and again a thunder shower drove them for shelter to the greenhouse where they waited while the hailstones rattled on the glass roof.

'Why should you mind going away, since you never see him?'

'I may not see him, but I know that he is there, living and breathing, only six miles away. When the wind blows from the east, I realize that he and I can hear the church bells at the very same moment. Would it make no difference to you whether Bernard were in Argelouse or Paris? I don't *see* Jean, but I have the certainty that he is not far off. At Sunday Mass I don't even bother to turn round because from where we sit we can see only the altar, and there's a pillar between us and the rest of the congregation: but on the way out ...'

'He wasn't there last Sunday, was he?'

Thérèse had been accurately informed. She knew that Anne, following dutifully in her mother's wake, had sought in vain among the crowd for the face that was not there.

'He may have been ill. ... They stop his letters: there's no way I can get news of him.'

'All the same, it seems odd that he shouldn't have found some way of sending a message to you.'

'Oh, Thérèse, if only *you*! ... Of course, I know how difficult your position is, but ...'

'Agree to take this trip, and perhaps, while you're away ...'

'I can't leave him.'

'But in any case *he'll* be going away. In a few weeks now he'll leave Argelouse.'

'Don't talk like that ... I can't bear even to think of it! Not a word from him to help me go on living! I'm more than half dead already as a result of the long silence. I have to remind myself, every moment, of all the things he said which made me really happy. I repeat them over and over to myself – so often, indeed, that I end by wondering whether he ever actually said them at all. I can hear his voice now, the way it sounded the last time we met. "You're the only person in my life I care two hoots about," he said – at least, I think that was it, though it may have been "You're the most precious thing I have in life. ..." I don't remember the exact words.'

She stood there frowning, striving to catch the echo of that spoken consolation, endlessly elaborating its meaning.

'What is he really like?'

'You can have no idea ...'

'So unlike everybody else?'

'I wish I could describe him, but no words of mine could ever paint his portrait. ... He might, I suppose, seem quite ordinary to you ... though I'm almost sure he wouldn't.'

It was quite beyond her power to get a clear view of the young man who shone resplendent in the bright radiance of her love. 'Passion,' thought Thérèse, 'would made me clearer-sighted. I should take note of every detail in the man whom I desired.'

'If I agree to go on this trip, Thérèse, will you see him? Will you tell me what he says? Will you give him my letters? If I go away, if I pluck up courage enough to go away ...'

Making her way from that kingdom of light and fire, Thérèse plunged again, like a dark wasp, into the room where mother and father were waiting for the heat to abate and their daughter to surrender. Only after many of these comings and goings did Anne finally make up her mind to agree. It was not so much the efforts of Thérèse as the imminent return of the Deguilheims that finally prevailed. She trembled at the thought of this new danger. Thérèse had kept on saying that, for a tremendously rich young man, the Deguilheim boy wasn't 'really half bad'.

'I've hardly ever looked at him properly, Thérèse. All I know is that he wears spectacles, is going bald, and is an old man.'

'He is twenty-nine. ...'

'That's what I mean – an old man. But old or not ...'

At dinner that evening the de la Traves mentioned Biarritz, and began fussing about hotels. Thérèse kept her eyes fixed on Anne. The girl sat perfectly still: she seemed emptied of all vitality.

'Do make just a tiny effort ... one can always eat if only one tries,' Madame de la Trave kept on saying. Anne lifted the spoon to her mouth. Her eyes looked quite dead. The one person who was not there, alone had any existence for her. There was nothing, nobody, in her life save only he. At moments a smile flickered on her lips as she remembered something he had said, some kiss he had given her in those distant days when, in a hut of turves, his clumsy hands had undone the first few buttons of her blouse. Thérèse looked away, concentrating her eyes on Bernard leaning over his plate. He was seated against the light, and she could not see his face. But she could hear the sound he made as he chewed the food by which he set such store, like some ruminant cow. She got up and left the table. Her mother-in-law said:

'She'd rather one didn't notice her. I'd cosset her if she'd let me, but she hates being fussed over. Considering her condition, she's not having too bad a time. She smokes too much, but it's no use telling her.' The old lady fell into a series of reminiscences to do with child-bearing. 'I remember when I was expecting you I had to sniff at a rubber ball. It was the only thing that kept me from being sick.'

'Thérèse, where are you?'

'Here, on the bench.'

'So you are; I can see your cigarette.'

Anne sat down, rested her head against an unyielding shoulder, looked at the sky, and remarked:

'He is gazing at those same stars, hearing the same Angelus bell. ...' Then, after a pause: 'Give me a kiss, Thérèse.' But Thérèse made no effort to bend down to the trusting face beside her. She merely said:

'Are you miserable?'

'No, not this evening. I realize that somehow, somewhere, we shall be together again. I feel quite calm now. The only really important thing is that he should know – and you'll see to that. I have made up my mind to go on this trip. But when I get back walls shall not keep me from him. Sooner or later I shall lie against his heart. I am as sure of that as I am of my own existence. No, Thérèse, don't *you* start preaching and talking about the family. ...'

'I wasn't thinking about the family, darling: I was thinking about him. It's not so easy to worm one's way into a man's life. He, too, has a family, work, interests – there may even be another woman. ...'

'There isn't. He said, "You're the only person in my life"; and, another time, "Our love is the only thing that means anything at all now. ..."'

'Now?'

'What are you hinting? Do you think that by "now" he meant just at this particular moment?'

There was no need for Thérèse to ask again whether she were miserable. She could hear the sounds of her misery in the darkness. But she felt no pity. How sweet it must be to say a name over and over, the pet name of the man to whom one's heart is tightly bound! – merely to think he is alive and breathing; that he sleeps at night with his head upon his arm, and wakes at dawn; that his young body plunges through the morning mist ...

'You're crying, Thérèse! Is it because of me? Do you love me?'

The girl had slipped to her knees. For a while she stayed so, her head pressed against Thérèse's side. Suddenly she got up.

'I felt something moving against my forehead: something, I don't know what. ...'

'He started moving some days ago.'

'The baby?'

'Yes; he's alive already.'

They went back to the house, their arms round one another's waist, as in the old days on the road to Nizan, on the road to Argelouse. Thérèse remembered how frightened she had been of this twittering burden. What passions might not force an entry into the still unformed flesh within her womb! She could see herself now as she had sat that evening in her room, before the open window. (Bernard had called up to her from the garden, 'Don't put on the light: it will attract the mosquitoes.') She had reckoned the months that remained before the child would be born. She longed to have knowledge of some God. She wanted to pray that this unknown life which was still an undistinguishable part of herself might never see the light of day.

6

It is strange that Thérèse remembered the days which followed the departure of Anne and her parents only as a time of torpor. At Argelouse, where it had been agreed that she should seek the joint in young Azévédo's armour and force him to relinquish his hold, she longed only for rest and sleep. Bernard had agreed that they should live, not in his house, but in hers, which was more comfortable, and where Aunt Clara could take over all the cares of housekeeping. Other people meant nothing now to Thérèse. They could look after themselves. Until the child should come she wanted nothing but to be left in her state of dull, animal languor. Each morning, Bernard irritated her by recalling her promise that she would arrange a meeting with the young man. She snubbed him for his pains. She was beginning to find it increasingly difficult to put up with him. It may have been, as Bernard thought, that her condition had something to do with her mood. He himself was already showing signs of an obsession which frequently afflicts the men of his race, though it rarely shows itself in persons under thirty. It was curious to find the fear of death so strongly developed in anyone who was, to all seeming, as strong as a horse. But what answer could she make when he said: 'Can't you realize what I'm suffering? ...' The bodies of these heavy eaters, bred of a lazy, over-nourished race, have only the appearance of sturdiness. A pine-tree planted in the rich soil of a field grows quickly: but its heart rots quickly too, and in its prime it has to be cut down. 'It's just nerves,' she told him; but was conscious of the weak spot, of the flaw, in the metal. And then the most extraordinary, the most inconceivable thing happened – he gave up eating, lost his appetite. 'Why don't you see a doctor?' He shrugged his shoulders at that and assumed an air of indifference. The truth was, he preferred his present state of uncertainty to a possible sentence of death. At night, Thérèse, would sometimes be jerked awake by a rattling sound in his throat. His hand would seek hers and press it to his left side that she might feel how irregularly his heart was beating. Then she would light a candle, get up and pour a few drops of tincture of valerian into a glass of water. What bad luck it was, she thought, that this draught should have the effect of relieving him. How much better if it turned out to be a mortal dose. Eternity is your only genuine guarantee of peace and quiet. Why should this whining creature at her side be so frightened of what would set his fears at rest for ever? He fell asleep before she did. How could she expect to drop off into unconsciousness with that great body in the bed beside her, its heavy breathing turning at times to a choking struggle? Thank God, though, he left her alone now – having come to the conclusion that love-making was the worst possible thing for his heart.

The cocks of dawn wakened the farmsteads. The sound of the Angelus came to her on the east wind from Saint-Clair, and then, at long last, sleep closed her eyes, just as he was struggling back to life. He dressed quickly, putting on old country clothes (his washing consisted in no more than wetting his face with cold water). Then he crept like a dog into the kitchen, greedy for the larder scraps. He breakfasted off what remained of last night's meat, or perhaps a hunk of cold paté, or grapes and a piece of bread rubbed with garlic – his only solid meal of the day. What was left over he threw to Flambeau and Diane, who snapped at the food. The mist had in it the smell of autumn. At that hour he no longer felt like a sick man, but was conscious once again of his old youthful vigour. Soon the duck would be on the wing. He must see to the decoy birds, put out their eyes.

When he returned at eleven o'clock he found Thérèse still in bed.

'What about young Azévédo? You know that mother is waiting for news of him – poste restante, Biarritz?'

'How's your heart?'

'Please leave my heart alone! Talking about my symptoms makes me conscious of them ... which only goes to show that it's nerves, really ... You think it is just nerves, don't you?'

She never gave him the answer he wanted.

'One can never be altogether sure. You're the only person who can know how you feel. ... But just because your father died of angina pectoris, that's no reason ... especially at your age ... Obviously, the heart is the Achilles heel of the Desqueyroux family. What an odd creature you are, Bernard, with your constant fear of death! Do you never have a feeling, as I do, of utter futility? No? Doesn't it occur to you that the sort of life people like us lead is remarkably like death?'

He shrugged his shoulders. Her paradoxes bored him. It is
not particularly clever to be witty. All one has got to do is to
take the ordinary, sensible person's point of view and turn
it upside down. Why waste her gifts on him? he said. Much
better keep them for young Azévédo when she saw him.

'You know that he's leaving Vilméja about the middle of
October?'

At Villandraut, the station before Saint-Clair, Thérèse
thought: 'How can I ever get Bernard to believe that I wasn't
in love with that young man? I'm sure he thinks that I adored
him. Like all those who really know nothing whatever about
love, he imagines that a crime of the sort with which I was
charged could have had its motive only in sexual passion.'
Bernard must be made to see that at the period in question
she was still far from hating him, tiresome though she often
found his importunity. No other man would have been of the
slightest use to her. When all was said, Bernard wasn't so
bad. There was nothing she detested more in novels than the
delineation of extraordinary people who had no resemblance
to anyone whom one met in normal life.

Her father had been the only truly remarkable man she had
ever known. She must give that headstrong, suspicious radical
the credit of being built on heroic lines. His activities were
numberless. He combined the functions of a landed pro-
prietor and industrialist (in addition to his sawmills at B—,
he handled the resin from his own trees and from those of his
innumerable relations in a factory at Saint-Clair). But above
all else, he was a man of politics. Though his cavalier way of
dealing with others had done him no little harm, he still had
the ear of the authorities. And how contemptuous he was of
women! – even of Thérèse, at a time when everyone was
praising her intelligence. The recent dramatic happenings
had strengthened him in his opinion. 'Hysterical, all of 'em,
when they're not fools!' he had said to her Counsel. For all
his anti-clericalism, he was a thorough-paced Puritan. He
might occasionally hum a song of Béranger's, but he would
blush like a boy if certain subjects were so much as mentioned

in his hearing. Bernard had been told by Monsieur de la Trave that Larroque had been completely innocent when he married: 'and it's common knowledge that he's never had a mistress since his wife died. Your father's a character if ever there was one!' Yes, he certainly was that. But though Thérèse, away from him, was inclined to touch up his portrait a bit, she had only to see him again to realize what a mean, vulgar creature he was. He came seldom to Saint-Clair, though more frequently to Argelouse, because he disliked meeting the de la Traves. Whenever they were present, though politics were barred, the same idiotic old quarrel inevitably began with the soup, and rapidly became embittered. Thérèse would have been ashamed to join in it. She felt it a matter of pride not to open her lips on those occasions, unless the talk turned to religion. Whenever that happened, she flung herself into the fray in her father's support. Everyone talked at the tops of their voices, making so much noise that even Aunt Clara managed to catch an occasional word and proceeded to join in the altercation. In her terrible deaf old voice she gave free rein to her radical fanaticism. *She* knew, she said, what went on in Convents, though at heart (thought Thérèse) she was a more sincere believer than any of the de la Trave clan. It was only that she waged incessant warfare against the Eternal Being who had let her become deaf and ugly, who had decreed that she should die without ever having been loved or possessed by a man. But ever since the day when Madame de la Trave had left the table they had entered into a tacit agreement to avoid all metaphysical discussion. But politics were quite enough to set them all by the ears, though fundamentally, whether their sympathies were of the Right or the Left, they were all in complete agreement on one point – that property is the most solid good this life can show, and that the only true value of existence is in earthly possessions. The sole question at issue was, should one or should one not set some limit to the acquisitive instincts, and, if so, where was it to be? Thérèse, who had the 'sense of property in her blood', would have preferred that they should face the question in a spirit of cynicism. What she hated was the sham air of righteousness with which the Larroques and the de la Traves attempted to disguise this shared passion. When her father announced that he was 'unshakably loyal to the principles of democracy,' she would interrupt him with, 'You needn't bother to talk like that here: we're quite alone, you know.' She said that all this highfalutin political posturing made her feel positively sick. The tragedy of the class-war was never really forced on her attention in a countryside where even the poorest have *some* property, and are for ever striving to amass more; where a common love of the soil, of shooting, of food, and of drink, creates between all – middle and labouring class alike – a close bond of brotherhood. But Bernard had, in addition, some degree of education. The neighbours said of him that he had got out of his rut, and even Thérèse took pleasure in the thought that he was the kind of man with whom it was possible to carry on some sort of rational conversation, a man who had 'risen superior to his environment ...' or so she regarded him until she met Jean Azévédo.

It was that time of year when the freshness of the night hours persists all through the morning: when, from luncheon on, no matter how hot the sun has been, a hint of mist announces the oncoming of darkness. The first of the duck were already flying, and Bernard scarcely ever came home before nightfall. On the particular day in question, however, he had decided, after sleeping badly, to go straight into Bordeaux and get himself examined by a doctor.

'I had no conscious wish at all,' thought Thérèse, looking back on the event. 'I used to take an hour's stroll every day up the road, because exercise is good for a woman when she's breeding. I avoided the woods because the shooting season had begun, which meant constantly stopping and whistling to announce one's presence, and waiting until one of the guns gave a shout to show that the coast was clear. But sometimes there would come an answering whistle which meant that a covey had settled in the trees. When that happened one had to lie low. Later, I would go back home and doze in front of the fire, either in the drawing-room or the kitchen, and let Aunt

Clara busy herself with doing little odds and ends for me. She was for ever droning on about household or farm matters, but I took no more notice of her than God does of his servants. She never stopped talking, because she didn't want to make the effort needed to hear other people. Almost always her soliloquies took the form of squalid stories about the country folk whom she looked after and watched over with a devotion which was completely disillusioned – stories of old men slowly starving to death, condemned to work until they could work no longer, abandoned by their relations and left to die, or of women forced to undertake the most exhausting labours. They would say the most frightful things, and these Aunt Clara would repeat almost gaily, just like a child. The one person she really loved was me, and yet I scarcely even noticed her when she got down on her knees to unlace my boots, take off my stockings, and warm my feet in her old hands.

'Balion used to come for orders the evening before he was due to go into Saint-Clair. Aunt Clara would make out a list of errands for him, entrusting him with the various prescriptions needed for the sick of Argelouse. "I want you to go first of all to the chemist. It'll take Darquey a long time to make up all these. ..."

'My first meeting with Jean. ... I want to get each detail clear in my mind. I had decided to go to the lonely hut where Anne and I used to eat our little snacks, and where I knew she had later loved to meet young Azévédo. I didn't regard it in the light of a sentimental pilgrimage. What took me there was the knowledge that the trees had grown too big to make birdwatching easy, and that, consequently, I ran little risk of disturbing the guns. The hut was no longer used for shooting because the forest all around blotted out the horizon. There were no long, open drives in which it was possible to follow the movement of the coveys. The October sun was still hot. The sandy path hurt my feet, the flies plagued me. How heavy my body felt! I longed to sit down on the rotting bench in the hut. I opened the door, and a young man came out. He was bareheaded. I recognized him at first sight. It was Jean Azévédo, and he looked so confused that I thought I might have interrupted some amorous tryst. I tried to get away, but in vain. Oddly enough, he seemed intent on keeping me there. "Please come in," he said. "You're not disturbing me at all; truly you're not."

'He was so insistent that I went into the hut, and was surprised to find nobody there. Perhaps the country girl whose presence I suspected had made good her escape by another exit. But no twig had snapped. He, too, had recognized me and began to talk of Anne de la Trave. I had sat down, but he remained standing just as I had seen him in the snapshot. My eyes sought, through the silk shirt, the spot where I had pierced him with my pin. There was no touch of passion in my glance, only a cold curiosity. Was he good-looking? He had a high forehead and the eyes of his race. His cheeks were too full, and he was afflicted with what I most dislike in young men, pimples, those signs of the sappy movement of the blood that speak of unwholesomeness. Worst of all, he had moist palms which he dried with his handkerchief before shaking my hand. But there was fire in the depths of his fine eyes, and I liked the wide mouth, which was never quite shut, and the sharp teeth. It reminded me of the muzzle of a young dog suffering from the heat. And how did I behave? I was very family-conscious, I remember, and took a high line with him from the first, accusing him, rather solemnly, of "bringing discord into a respectable home". There was nothing assumed about his amazement. He laughed in my face. "Do you really believe that I want to marry her? that I aspire to such a prize as that?" I was dumbfounded when I realized, as I did at once, the gulf which existed between Anne's passionate adoration and this young man's complete indifference. He defended himself hotly. How could he help, he said, yielding to the charms of so delightful a child? Where was the harm in having a bit of fun? Just because there never had been any question of marriage between them, it had all seemed to him perfectly legitimate. Of course he had pretended to fall in with her views. By this time I was mounted on my high horse,

57

but when I interrupted him he started off again more urgently than ever. Anne would tell me herself that he had never gone too far. Of one thing he was quite certain, that he had probably given Mademoiselle de la Trave the only chance she would ever have in her whole gloomy existence of tasting real passion. "You say she's miserable. But tell me honestly, do you think she can look forward to anything better than such misery? I know you by reputation. I know that one can speak frankly to you, that you're not like most of the people round here. She's all set for a dull life in some old house in Saint-Clair. At least I have given her feeling and dreams to hoard up against her old age – something to save her from despair, perhaps, and certainly from becoming stupid and unimaginative." I can't remember whether I was exasperated by this monstrous piece of affectation, or whether I even noticed it. Truth to tell, he spoke so fast that at first I had considerable difficulty in following him, though after a while my mind adjusted itself to his spate of words. "Was it likely that I should contemplate such a marriage, should drop anchor in such shifting sands, or saddle myself in Paris with a little girl like that? I shall always remember Anne as a delightful incident in my life – as a matter of fact, I was thinking of her when you came on me so suddenly. But how can anyone dream of tying himself up for good? One should be in a position to suck the last drop of pleasure from each fleeting moment – and every pleasure is different from those that have gone before." This greediness, as of a young animal, this sudden discovery of *one* intelligent person, seemed to me so strange that I listened to what he had to say without making any attempt to interrupt him. I was completely dazzled – pretty easily, I admit: but the fact remains that I was. I remember the pattering of hooves, the tinkling of bells, the wild cries of shepherds in the distance, which told of an approaching flock. I told the young man that it might seem rather strange if we were found alone together in the hut. I should have liked him to reply that we had better not make a sound until the flock had passed. I should have enjoyed staying there with him in complete silence, should have relished the sense of guilty complicity (for I, too, was becoming exigent, was beginning to demand that each minute bring something to live for), but Jean Azévédo opened the door without a word of protest and, after ceremoniously taking leave, stood back for me to pass. He followed me to Argelouse only after making quite certain that I had no objection to his doing so. How quickly the time passed, though my companion managed to touch on a thousand different subjects. In an odd sort of way he gave a new freshness to things with which I had long been familiar – to the question of religion, for instance. When I repeated the kind of thing I was used to saying in the family circle, he broke in with: "No doubt that's true enough, but it's all really a great deal more complicated. ..." He brought to the argument a clearness of vision which I could not help admiring. ... But was it so admirable, after all? ... I feel pretty sure that today my stomach would reject such a mixed dish. He told me he had long believed that the only really important thing was to seek God and strive after Him. "All that matters is to hoist one's sails and make for the open sea, avoiding like the plague all those who persuade themselves that they have found what they sought, who cease to move forward, but build their little shelters and compose themselves to slumber. I have long mistrusted all such people. ..."

'He asked whether I had read René Bazin's *La Vie du Père de Foucauld*, and when I gave him a mocking answer assured me that the book had completely knocked him sideways. "To live dangerously, in the fullest sense of the word, that's what ought to be one's object. It's not so much seeking God that matters, as, having once found him, to remain within his orbit." He described to me the "great adventure of the mystics," and bewailed the fact that he was not temperamentally suited to follow in their steps. As far back as he could remember, he said, he had never been pure. How different was such immodesty, such facile self-confession, from the scrupulous wariness of my country neighbours, from the silence with which, at home, we surrounded the secrets of our personal lives! The gossips of Saint-Clair move only on the surface of things: one never sees into their hearts. What do

I really know of Bernard? Surely there must be a lot more to him than the caricature of a man with which I have to rest content whenever I feel tempted to conjure up his image? Jean did all the talking and I remained silent. Nothing came to my lips but the habitual phrases of which I made use in our family arguments. Just as in this part of the country all carriages are precisely "fitted to the road", or, in other words, just wide enough to ensure that the wheels will fit neatly into the ruts made by the passing waggons, so all my thoughts, till that moment, had been equally "fitted to the road" which my father and my parents-in-law had traced. Jean Azévédo walked bareheaded. I can see again his open shirt and the glimpse it gave of a chest which might have been that of a child, and of his rather over-developed neck. Had I fallen a victim to his physical charms? Good heavens, no! But he was the first man I had met for whom the life of the mind meant everything. His masters, his Paris friends – whose sayings and whose books he constantly quoted to me – made it impossible to regard him as in any way exceptional. He was just one of a numerous *élite* – "the people who are really alive", he called them. He mentioned names. It did not occur to him for a single moment that I might never have heard of them – and I pretended that I was not now making their acquaintance for the first time.

'When, at a turn in the road, we saw before us the Argelouse paddock, I exclaimed, "Back already!" Smoke from the scorched grass hung low over the poor soil from which the rye crop had already been lifted. Through a gap in the bank a flock of sheep was winding its way, looking like dirty milk, and apparently browsing on the sand. Jean had to cross the paddock in order to reach Vilméja. I said: "I'm coming with you: I'm wildly interested in all these questions." But we found no more to say. The rye stubble hurt my feet through the thin soles of my shoes. I had a feeling that he wanted to be alone, no doubt in order to pursue at leisure some line of thought which had presented itself to his mind. I pointed out to him that we had not spoken of Anne. He answered that we were not free to choose the subject of our conversation, or even of our thoughts. "One can do that," he added with a little show of arrogance, "only if one submits to the discipline invented by the mystics. ... People like us always float with the current, go where the slope leads. ..." In this way he brought back our talk to the books he was reading at the moment. We arranged to meet again in order to draw up a plan of campaign about Anne. He spoke absent-mindedly, and, without answering some question I had put to him, suddenly bent down. With a childlike gesture he pointed to a mushroom growing there, sniffed at it, and put it to his lips.'

7

WHEN she got back she had found Bernard waiting for her on the doorstep. 'There's nothing wrong with me!' he had cried, as soon as he caught a glimpse of her dress in the half-light; 'nothing at all — except, believe it or not, that I'm anaemic, a big, hulking fellow like me. Appearances, it seems, are deceptive. I've got to have a course of treatment – Fowler ... it's got arsenic in it, you know. The important thing is that I should get back my appetite. ...'

Thérèse remembered that at first she had felt no irritation. Bernard's affairs seemed to make less impression on her than usual (it was as though someone had fired at long range, and missed her). She barely heard him. She seemed caught up, body and mind, into an entirely different world, a place of eager beings whose sole desire was to know and understand; to be 'themselves', as Jean had said more than once with an air of deep satisfaction. Later, as they sat at their meal, and she brought herself to mention the afternoon's meeting, Bernard exclaimed: 'You *are* an odd creature! And what have you decided?'

She proceeded, there and then, to improvise the plan which was, in fact, the one they carried out. Jean Azévédo had agreed to write a letter to Anne in which, as gently as possible, he would kill any hope that she might have entertained. Bernard laughed sceptically when she insisted that the young man set no store whatever by such a marriage. What! an Azévédo not care whether he married an Anne de la Trave or not? 'You must be mad! The truth of the matter is that he knows there's nothing doing. Chaps of his kidney won't take risks when they know that they are bound to lose. You're still very innocent, my dear!'

Because of the mosquitoes, he had been unwilling to have the lamp lighted. Consequently, he could not see the expression of her face. He had 'recovered his appetite', as he put it. Already the Bordeaux doctor had given him a new lease of life.

'Did I see much more of Jean Azévédo? ... He left Argelouse towards the end of October. We may have gone walking together five or six times. The only occasion of which I have any clear recollection is the one on which we composed the letter he was to send to Anne. He was not a very experienced young man, and used expressions which he thought would allay her fears, though I knew perfectly well how horrible she would find them. Our last expeditions are all mixed up in a single memory. Jean Azévédo described Paris to me, and the friends he had there. I imagined a sort of a realm in which the only law was "be thyself".

' "Here you are condemned to a life of deceit until you die." Did he say that deliberately? What did he suspect? I should find it impossible, according to him, to breathe so stifling an atmosphere. "Look," he said, "at the vast, smooth surface of ice beneath which the minds of all here are frozen. Through an occasional hole the water shows black. That means that someone has disappeared after a violent struggle. But the crust re-forms above it. ... For each man, here as elsewhere, is born subject to the law of his nature: here, as elsewhere, individual destiny rules each single life. It is no good kicking against the pricks. But some do, and that accounts for those petty dramas which the various families agree to keep shrouded in silence. As they say hereabouts, 'Not a word ...' "

' "How right you are!" I exclaimed. "There have been times when I have asked about some great-uncle, or about some woman of an older generation, whose photographs have been removed from the family album: but the only answer I have ever got is: 'He took himself off ... it was arranged that he should. ...' "

'Did Jean Azévédo fear some such fate for me? He said that it would never occur to him to talk of these matters to Anne because, in spite of her passionate nature, she was really a very simple little soul. There was not much fight in her. She would quickly toe the line. "But you're different! In your every word I can detect a hunger and thirst after sincerity. ..." Need I tell Bernard all the things he said? It was madness to hope that my husband would be capable of even understanding them! But I must make him see that I did not surrender without a struggle. I remember arguing with Jean, telling him that he was merely dressing up the worst kind of moral depravity in high-sounding phrases. I even had recourse to the copybook maxim which lingered on in my memory from schooldays. "Be thyself," I said. "But we are what we are only in so far as we make our own characters." (Unnecessary to develop the thought now, though I might have to do so later for Bernard's benefit.) Jean Azévédo denied that there could be any depravity worse than the denial of self. He maintained that heroes and saints habitually struck a balance-sheet of their natures, that they became what they were only because they realized their limitations. "If one is to find God one must transcend one's limitations," he kept on saying. And, on another occasion: "Accepting ourselves for what we are forces each one of us to come to grips with his real nature, to see it clearly and engage it in mortal combat. That is why so many emancipated minds become converted to religion in its narrowest forms."

'I shall not discuss with Bernard the rights and wrongs of such a moral doctrine: I'm even prepared to subscribe to his view that it doubtless contains much wretched sophistry. But he must understand, must make himself understand, just how a woman of my sort could be irritated by the life we led, just what she felt on those evenings in the dining-room at Argelouse when he was taking off his boots in the kitchen next door, and regaling me the while, in a rich local dialect, with talk of the day's happenings. I can see it all now: the captive birds struggling in the bag on the table, distending it with their movements, and Bernard eating slowly, relishing his recovered appetite, counting with loving care the "Fowler" drops, and saying, while he did so, "This is what is making me well." A great fire used to be burning on the hearth, and he had only to turn his chair to be able to stretch his slippered feet to the blaze. He would nod over *la Petite Gironde*. Sometimes he snored, but there were times too, when I scarcely heard him breathe. Old Madame Balion's clogs would sound on the kitchen flags, and she would appear with the candles. All around us was the silence: the silence of Argelouse! People who have never lived in that lost corner of the heath-country can have no idea what silence means. It stands like a wall about the house, and the house itself seems as though it were set solid in the dense mass of the forest, whence comes no sign of life, save occasionally the hooting of an owl. (At night I could almost believe that I heard the sob I was at such pains to stifle.)

'It was after Azévédo had gone that I got to know that silence. So long as I was sure that he would come to me with the new day the thought of his presence robbed the smothering dark of all its terrors. The fact that he was lying asleep near by gave me a feeling that the night and all the sweep of moorland was rich with life. But when he left Argelouse after that last meeting at which he arranged that we should meet in a year's time, and was full of hope (he said) that when the day came I should have found some way of freeing myself (I still don't know whether he threw that out lightheartedly or whether there was some idea at the back of his mind. I have an impression that, being a bred-in-the-bone Parisian, he could not bear the silence, the particular silence of Argelouse, any longer, and that he adored me simply and solely because I was his one and only audience) – when I saw the last of him, I felt as though I had plunged into an endless tunnel, that I was driving ahead into a darkness which grew more dense the farther I advanced, so that I sometimes wondered whether I should suffocate before I reached the open air again.

'But until my labours began in January nothing happened ...'

At this point Thérèse began to hesitate, forcing her mind from brooding on what had occurred in the house at Argelouse on the day after Jean's departure. 'No,' she thought, 'that has nothing whatever to do with what I've got to explain to Bernard when we meet. I have no time to waste wandering up blind alleys.' But the mind is impatient of discipline. We cannot prevent it from roaming at will. She completely failed to blot that October evening from her memory. Upstairs, on the first floor, Bernard was undressing. She was waiting until the last of the fire should have died down before joining him, happy to be left alone even for a minute. What was Jean Azévédo doing? Perhaps he was drinking in the little bar of which he had told her: perhaps (for the night was mild) he was driving in his car with a friend through the deserted Bois de Boulogne; perhaps he was sitting at his table, working, with the Paris traffic rumbling a distant accompaniment. If there was silence about him, it was of his own creation, a little niche of peace hollowed out of the hubbub of the world: not forced on him from without, like the silence in which Thérèse sat suffocating. His was the achievement of a determined will, though it reached no farther than the circle of lamplight and the packed bookshelves.

... So her mind worked, and then the dog barked, and followed the bark with a whimper, as a well-known voice, speaking in tones of utter exhaustion from somewhere in the hall, quieted him.

Anne de la Trave opened the door. She had walked all the way from Saint-Clair in the dark and her shoes were clotted with mud. In her face – which had grown much older – the eyes shone bright. She flung her hat into an arm-chair. 'Where is he?' she said.

Once the famous letter had been written and posted, Thérèse and Jean had regarded the whole affair as being over and done with. It never occurred to them that Anne might find it impossible to let go her hold: How could anyone be expected to yield to the promptings of reason or the force of logic when her whole life was at stake? She had managed to escape her mother's vigilance, and to take a train. On the dark road to Argelouse she had been guided by the strips of clear sky which showed between the trees. The only thing that mattered was that she should see him again. If only she could be at his side he *must* yield once more to her charm. She had *got* to see him. She stumbled in her haste to reach Argelouse. Her feet caught in the ruts. And now, here was Thérèse telling her that he had gone, that he was back in Paris. She shook her head in denial, refusing to believe it. If she did not refuse to believe it she would faint from weariness and despair.

'You're lying to me: you've always lied to me.'

Thérèse protested, but the girl went on:

'You're just like all the rest of the family ... for all your emancipated airs. ... As soon as you married you became just another woman of the same old lot. I know you meant well. You betrayed me for my own good, didn't you? Don't bother to explain; I know exactly what you're going to say.'

She opened the door again. Thérèse asked where she was going.

'To Vilméja, to his home.'

'But he hasn't been there for the past two days. I've told you that already.'

'I don't believe you.'

She left the room. Thérèse lit the lantern which hung in the hall, and followed her.

'You're going wrong, Anne dear. That's the way to Biourge; Vilméja's in the other direction.'

They walked on through the mist which was drifting up from the fields. Dogs woke as they passed. At length they saw the oaks of Vilméja, and the house itself, not sleeping now but dead. Anne wandered round the empty sepulchre. She beat on the door with her two fists. Thérèse stood there motionless. She had set the lantern on the grass. She saw the faint outline of her friend as she flattened herself against each ground-floor window. No doubt she was saying that one name over and over again, though not aloud, for what good would that have done? For a moment or two the house hid her. Then she reappeared, reached the door once more, and sank down on the threshold, clasping her arms about her knees, hiding her face. Thérèse raised her up and led her away. The girl, stumbling as she went, kept on saying: 'Tomorrow morning I shall go to Paris. Paris is large, but I shall find him all right. ...' She spoke like a child at the end of its tether, and as though she were already emptied of all hope.

Bernard, who had been awakened by the sound of their voices, was waiting for them in the drawing-room, wrapped in a dressing-gown. It was a mistake on Thérèse's part to turn her mind from the memory of the scene which flared up between brother and sister. This man, who could seize an exhausted young girl by the wrists, drag her upstairs, and lock her in her room, is your husband, that same Bernard who, in two hours' time, will be your judge. The spirit of the family inspires his every action, making it impossible for him to hesitate even for a moment. Always, in every circumstance, he knows what must be done in the interests of the family. You dread the meeting: you are busy preparing a detailed defence. But only men without strong principles can yield to the unexpected argument. Bernard will laugh at your carefully reasoned defence. 'I know what's got to be done.' He always knows what's got to be done. If, at times, he finds himself hesitating, he says: 'We discussed all that at a family council, and we've made up our minds. ...' Sentence has already been pronounced upon you: how can you doubt it? Your fate has been irremediably determined. You might just as well go to sleep.

8

WHEN the de la Traves had overcome Anne's resistance and taken her back to Saint-Clair, Thérèse remained at Argelouse until her child was due to be born. She learned to know every

67

feature of its silence during those endless November nights. She had written a letter to Jean Azévédo, but it remained unanswered. Clearly, he thought it not worth his while to embark on the tedium of a correspondence with a country girl. Besides, an expectant mother is never a very pleasant object to remember. Perhaps, now that he was away from her, he thought of her only as a drab little nonentity. The fool! Had she cared to indulge in trumped-up subtleties and scenes of melodrama, she could have held him easily enough! How could a man of his kind understand such deceptive simplicity as hers? How interpret her honest gaze and clear-cut certainty of gesture? Better face the truth. He believed that she, just as he had believed that the poor child Anne, was quite capable of taking him at his word, of leaving all and following him. Jean Azévédo was distrustful of women who throw down their arms before the enemy has even had the time to lay siege to them. He dreaded nothing so much as victory and the fruits of victory. Nevertheless, Thérèse forced herself to live in his mental world, though the books he admired (she had ordered them from Bordeaux) seemed to her utterly incomprehensible. How bored she was! There was no question of her filling the hours with making and sewing for the expected baby. That, said Madame de la Trave, 'was not her responsibility.' Many women living in the country die in childbirth. Thérèse made Aunt Clara cry by insisting that she would, as her mother had done before her: that she was sure she would not escape the fate hanging over her. Whenever she spoke like that, she was careful to add that she did not much care whether she lived or whether she didn't. But that was a lie. Never had she been so hungry for life, and never had Bernard shown himself more attentive. 'He wasn't concerned so much for me as for what I was carrying *in* me. He might drool on in that appalling brogue of his, "Now do eat up your mince ... you mustn't have any fish ... you've done quite enough walking for one day. ..." It no more affected me than a complaint about the quality of her milk affects a wet-nurse who has no particular interest in her employer's family. The de la Traves bestowed on me the same sort of regard as they would have done on a sacred vessel. I was just the container of their young. Had the necessity arisen, I am quite sure that they would have sacrificed me to my unborn child without a qualm. I lost all sense of being an individual person. In the eyes of the family I was merely a species of vine-shoot. All that mattered to them was the fruit of my womb.

'I had to go on living in that gloomy world until the end of December. As though there weren't enough pines already, the ceaseless rain built a million moving barriers about the darkened house. When it seemed likely that the single road to Saint-Clair would soon be impracticable, I was taken into the local town and settled into a house which was scarcely less overgrown and dark than Argelouse. The old plane-trees in the public Square were fighting with the rainy wind in an effort to keep their last few leaves. Aunt Clara, who could live nowhere but at Argelouse, refused to keep me company. But she braved the journey in all weathers, driving over to see me in her "just wide enough" gig. She brought me the little treats I had loved as a child, thinking that I loved them still – greyish lumps of honey and rye called "miques", the sort of cake known locally as "fougasse" or "roumadjade". I saw Anne only at meals, and she no longer spoke to me. She seemed to be cowed and resigned. Quite suddenly she had lost all her former freshness, and wore her hair drawn back so tightly that it left her rather ugly and anaemic ears plainly visible. Young Deguilheim's name was never mentioned, but Madame de la Trave asserted that if Anne had not yet said "yes" she at least was no longer saying "no". How right Jean had been about her. It had not taken long to break her in to harness. Bernard was less well than he had been, because he had started tippling again. What did all these people among whom I lived talk about? They discussed the Curé a good deal, I remember (the Presbytery was just opposite). There was much curiosity expressed, for instance, about why he had crossed the Square four times in one day, returning on each occasion by a different route. ...'

On account of something that Jean Azévédo had said,

Thérèse paid a good deal more attention to this young priest than she would otherwise have done. He had few points of contact with his parishioners. They thought him 'arrogant' – 'He's not the sort of man we need here.' On the rare occasions of his visits to the de la Trave household, Thérèse studied his greying temples and high forehead. How did he spend his evenings? He had no friends. Why had he chosen the religious life? 'He is very scrupulous,' said Madame de la Trave. 'He makes his act of adoration every evening, but he lacks unction. He is not what *I* call pious, and he does nothing whatever about social work.' She deplored the fact that he had done away with all ostentation of charity. The local parents, too, complained that he did not play football with the children. 'It's all very well to bury one's nose in books all day long; but a man can very soon lose his hold on a parish.' Thérèse went regularly to church in order to hear him preach. 'You've chosen just the moment, my dear, when you might well be excused from all such duties by reason of your condition.'

The Curé's sermons on points of dogma and morals were completely impersonal. But Thérèse was interested in the inflexions of his voice, in his gestures. At times he would lay particular stress on some one word. .... Ah! he, perhaps, might help her to come to terms with the confusion of her spirit. He was not like the people round her. He, too, had chosen the way of tragedy. To the solitude within he had added that desert which the soutane creates round those who wear it. What comfort did he find in the daily rites? She would have liked to be present at his weekday Masses, when, with only a single choirboy for congregation, he bent, murmuring, above a scrap of bread. But for her to have done so would have seemed odd to the members of her family and to the good people of the town. There would have been gossip about 'conversion'.

Though Thérèse's sufferings at that time may have been severe, it was only after the birth of her child that she really began to find life unendurable. Not that anything much happened. There were no scenes between her and Bernard.

She was more deferential to the parents even than he was. That there was no apparent reason for a break made the whole business more tragic. It seemed that nothing could possibly occur to disturb the flat routine of their days. They would go on just like this till they died. Disagreement presupposes the existence of a common ground on which the struggle can be waged. But Thérèse had no ground in common with Bernard, and still less with her mother- and father-in-law. Their words made no impression on her. It never occurred to her that she might be expected to answer when they spoke to her. They did not even share the same language, but attached totally different meanings to every essential word. Occasionally Thérèse might be goaded into an expression of sincerity. But it had no effect. The family had long ago agreed that she loved talking for talking's sake. 'I just pretend not to listen,' said Madame de la Trave; 'and, if she goes on, I look as though I didn't attach any importance to what she says. She knows that all that talk of hers does not impress *us*. ...'

All the same, Madame de la Trave found it hard to put up with Thérèse's affectation of annoyance when people said how like her little Marie was. The ordinary chatter customary on such occasions ('You'd know at once whose child *she* is!') threw the young mother into transports of irritability, and these she could not always conceal. 'There's nothing of me in the little creature!' she would insist. 'Look at her brown skin and jet-black eyes. Compare her with one of *my* early photographs. I was a pasty little girl.'

She had no wish for Marie to be like her, she wanted to have as little as possible in common with the scrap of flesh and blood which had issued from her body. It began to be said that the maternal instinct did not trouble her unduly. But Madame de la Trave maintained that she was fond of the child in her own funny way. 'It's no good expecting her to give her her bath or to change her nappies. She's not that sort of woman. But I've seen her sitting a whole evening by the child's cradle, and not smoking at all, just so as she could watch her sleeping. ... We have an excellent nurse, and then, you see, there's always Anne. Now, *she's* utterly different!

She'll make a wonderful mother, no doubt about that. ...'
It was true that, with a child in the house, Anne had begun to
live again. Women are always attracted by a cradle, but Anne
seemed to find some peculiarly profound happiness in dandling
the baby. In order to have free access to it, she had made her
peace with Thérèse, though nothing of their old affection
remained apart from their use of pet names and familiar
gestures. The girl dreaded especially lest Thérèse's maternal
jealousy might be aroused. 'The little darling is much more at
ease with me than with her. Whenever she sees me she gurgles.
The other day I was holding her in my arms, and she started
to howl when Thérèse tried to take her from me. She is so
much fonder of me that it sometimes makes me feel quite
embarrassed. ...'

But she need not have been. All through this period of her
life Thérèse felt as though she were completely detached from
everyone, the child included. She saw people and things, her
own body and even her own mind, in the form of a mirage,
as a sort of cloud suspended outside herself. In all this emptiness Bernard alone had a horrible, a frightening, reality, with
his fat paunch, his nasal drawl, his peremptory way of talking,
his self-complacency. Escape from her world? – but how and
whither? The beginning of the hot weather completely
exhausted her. No premonition came to warn her of what she
was about to do. What happened that year? She could remember no single incident, no quarrel, only that she had felt more
detestation of her husband than usual on the occasion of the
Corpus Christi procession which she had watched from behind
half-closed shutters. Bernard was almost the only man walking
behind the Canopy. Within a few moments the village street
became as completely deserted as though a lion and not a
lamb had been let loose. ... The inhabitants ran for shelter
so as to avoid the necessity of uncovering or kneeling. Once
the danger had passed, doors began to open one by one.
Thérèse stared at the Curé, who was walking with eyes almost
completely shut, bearing in his two hands the strange,
mysterious object. His lips were moving. To whom was he

talking with that look of suffering on his face? And then, suddenly, she saw behind him Bernard 'doing his duty'.

Week followed week without so much as a drop of rain. Bernard lived in constant terror of fire. He was suffering from his heart again. More than a thousand acres had been burned over at Louchats. 'If the wind had been from the north I should have lost my Balisac pines.' Thérèse was in a state of waiting for she knew not what to fall from the immutable sky. It would never rain again. One day the whole surrounding forest would crackle into flame, even the town itself would not be spared. Why was it that the heath villages never caught fire? It seemed to her unjust that it should always be the trees that the flames chose, never the human beings. In the family circle there was a never-ending discussion about what caused these disasters. Was it a discarded cigarette, or was it deliberate mischief? Thérèse liked to imagine that one of these nights she would get up, leave the house, reach the most inflammable part of the forest, throw away her cigarette, and watch the great column of smoke stain the dawn sky. ... But she drove the thought from her, for the love of pine-trees was in her blood. It was not them that she hated.

And now the moment had been reached at which she must look her act straight in the face. How could she explain it to Bernard? All she could do would be to take him, step by step, over the road she had travelled to it. It was the day on which a big fire had broken out towards Mano. Some men from the estate had come into the dining-room where the members of the family were eating a hurried luncheon. Some of them said that the blaze was a long way from Saint-Clair, others that the tocsin ought to be sounded. The smell of burning resin filled the stifling air, and the sun looked dirty. Thinking back, Thérèse could see Bernard sitting there with his head turned, listening to Balion's report on the situation, and quite forgetful of the fact that his great hairy hand was holding his bottle of 'Fowler' over a glass of water, into which the drops were falling all unnoticed. He swallowed the medicine at a single gulp, before Thérèse, over-powered by the heat, could warn him that he had taken twice his usual dose. Everyone except herself had left the table. She sat there cracking fresh almonds, indifferent to what was going on, wholly detached from the drama of the fire as from every drama except her own. The tocsin did not sound, and Bernard came back into the room. 'For once you were right not to get excited. The fire's way over at Mano.' Then: 'Did I take my drops?' he asked. Without waiting for her answer, he began shaking some more into his glass. She said nothing, partly because she was too lazy to speak, partly, too, no doubt, because she was tired. For what was she hoping at that moment? 'I just can't believe that I deliberately *planned* to say nothing.'

But when, that night, Bernard lay vomiting and moaning in his bed, and Dr Pédemay asked her what had happened, she told him nothing about what she had seen in the dining-room, though it would have been so easy, without in any way compromising herself, to have drawn the doctor's attention to the arsenic which Bernard was taking. She could have said something like 'I didn't really notice it at the time ... we were all so much distracted by the fire ... but I'm prepared to swear now that he took twice his usual dose. ...' But she remained silent. Had she even felt tempted to say anything? The act which, at luncheon, had already though she did not know it, started to germinate in her mind began then to emerge from the depths of her being into the light ... formless still, but struggling into consciousness.

When the doctor had gone she stood there looking at Bernard, who had at last dropped off to sleep. She thought: 'There is nothing to prove it was *that*. It might be an attack of appendicitis, though there are no other symptoms ... or a case of virulent influenza.' But two days later Bernard was up and about again. 'It looks as though it *was* that.' Thérèse could not have sworn it was, and she wanted to be sure. 'I did not feel that I had been the prey of a horrible temptation. It was simply that I was curious, and, if I was to satisfy my curiosity, there were certain risks that I had to take. The first occasion on which I put some Fowler drops into his glass

74

before he came into the room I remember saying to myself, "Just once, to clear my mind of uncertainty. I shall know now whether it really *was* that. Just this once – I won't ever do it again. ..." '

The train came to a halt, uttered a long whistle, and started to move again. Two or three lights showed in the darkness. Saint-Clair station. But there was nothing more at which Thérèse need peer and puzzle. The maw of her crime had swallowed her, had sucked her in, sucked her down. Bernard knew, just as well as she did, what had followed: the sudden return of his weakness, with Thérèse watching by him night and day, though she seemed to have no strength left, and was incapable of swallowing even a mouthful of food (she was so exhausted, indeed, that he had persuaded her to try the Fowler treatment herself, and she had actually got Dr Pédemay to give her the necessary prescription). Poor doctor! – so surprised at the greenish colour of Bernard's vomitings, finding it hard to believe that so great a discrepancy could exist between a sick man's pulse and his temperature. He had often, in cases of paratyphoid, met with a slow pulse combined with a high temperature, but what could it mean when a racing pulse went with a subnormal temperature? Toxic influenza, no doubt. That magic word 'influenza' was held to explain everything. Madame de la Trave played with the idea of calling in a well-known consultant, but did not wish to affront the doctor, who was an old friend. Besides, Thérèse feared the effect of such a step on Bernard. About the middle of August, however, after a more than usually alarming crisis, Pédemay himself suggested a second opinion. Fortunately, however, next day Bernard began to show signs of improvement, and three weeks later he was said to be well on the way to convalescence. 'That was a narrow escape for me,' said Pédemay. 'If the great man had got here in time all the credit for the cure would have gone to him.'

Bernard had himself moved to Argelouse, counting on the duck-shooting to set him to rights again. It was an exhausting time for Thérèse. A sharp attack of rheumatism had confined

Aunt Clara to her bed, and all the work of the house fell on the younger woman. She had two invalids to look after, as well as the child, and all the chores that were usually shouldered by Aunt Clara. She was only too glad to do what she could to take the sick woman's place with the poor of Argelouse. She went round the farms, saw that the doctor's instructions were obeyed, and bought the necessary medicines out of her own pocket. It never occurred to her that the empty house at Vilméja might be a cause of sorrow. She was no longer thinking about Jean Azévédo, nor, for that matter, about anybody else. She seemed tearing through a tunnel in utter loneliness. She had reached its darkest point. Like some panic-stricken animal, she felt only that she had got to get out of the blackness, out of the smoke, into the fresh air, as quickly as she possibly could.

At the beginning of September Bernard had had a bad relapse. He awoke one morning shivering, his legs useless and without feeling. What a nightmare the following days had been! A consultant had been brought from Bordeaux one evening by Monsieur de la Trave. He had examined the patient and then, for a while, said nothing. (Thérèse had held the lamp, and Madame Balion still remembers that she looked whiter than the sheets.) On the badly-lit landing, Pédemay, keeping his voice low lest Thérèse should overhear him, had explained to his colleague that Darquey, the chemist, had shown him two forged prescriptions. To one of them a criminal hand had added the words *Fowler Mixture*: the other contained pretty powerful doses of chloroform, digitalis, and aconite. Balion had given them to the chemist together with several others. Darquey, worried to death by the thought that he had supplied these dangerous drugs, had rushed off next morning to Pédemay. ... Yes, all these details were as familiar to Bernard as they were to Thérèse. An ambulance, hastily summoned, had taken him off to a hospital in Bordeaux, and from that moment he had begun to improve. Thérèse had remained alone at Argelouse. Despite her solitude, she had been conscious of the sound of many voices. She was like a trapped animal that hears the pack drawing close and lies exhausted after a gruelling chase. It was as though, within reach of her goal, her hand already stretched to touch it, she had been suddenly flung to the earth. Her legs had buckled beneath her. She could no longer keep her feet. One evening, towards the end of the winter, her father had come over. He begged her to clear herself of suspicion. There was still time to put everything to rights. Pédemay had agreed not to proceed with the charge: had pretended that he could not be sure that one of the prescriptions was not wholly in his own handwriting. He couldn't, he said, have ordered such strong doses of chloroform and digitalis, but then no traces of them had been found in the sick man's blood, and ...

Thérèse remembered that scene with her father. It had taken place at Aunt Clara's bedside. The room was lit by the flickering of a wood fire. Neither of them had wanted a lamp. She had explained, in the dull, flat voice of a child reciting a lesson (the lesson which she had rehearsed over and over again as she lay sleepless in her bed): 'I met a stranger on the road. He said that since I was sending someone in to Darquey's, he hoped I would consent to have a prescription made up for him. He owed money to Darquey, and didn't want to show his face in the man's shop. He promised to come and fetch the drugs from the house, but gave me neither his name nor his address....'

'You'll have to find a better story than that, Thérèse. I beg you, for the sake of the family, to do so. Wretched woman! you *must* do something!'

Over and over again old Larroque had upbraided her. The deaf old spinster, lying propped up on her pillows, and feeling that some mortal threat was hanging over Thérèse, had groaned: 'What's he saying? What does he want? Why is he being so horrible to you?'

She had summoned up sufficient strength to smile at her aunt. She had held her hand, and said again, like a small child reciting her catechism: 'It was a man I met on the road. It was too dark to see his face. He didn't tell me which of the farms he lived at.' Later, he had come one evening to fetch his medicines. Unfortunately, no one in the house had seen him.

77

9

SAINT-CLAIR at last. Thérèse was not recognized as she left
the train. While Balion was giving up her ticket she walked
round to the other side of the station and made her way between the wood-stacks to the road, where the trap was
waiting.

It had become, for her, a refuge. There was small risk that
anyone would meet them in the unmetalled lane. The whole
story of her past, so painfully reassembled, fell in ruins about
her. No jot nor tittle of her carefully rehearsed confession
remained. There was nothing that she could say in her defence, not so much as an explanation that she could give. The
easiest thing would be to say nothing, or, at least, to speak only
when she was questioned. What was there to fear? This night
would pass like other nights; tomorrow's sun would rise.
Whatever happened, she would come through. There could
be nothing worse in store for her than this feeling of utter
indifference, this sense of complete detachment which seemed
to have cut her off from the rest of the world, and even from
herself. Death in life. She was tasting death now as surely as
the living can ever do.

Her eyes grew accustomed to the darkness. At a turn in the
road she recognized a farm where the low outbuildings looked
like sleeping, crouching animals. It was here that, in the old
days, Anne had always been frightened of a dog which had a
way of jumping out at her bicycle wheel. A little farther on a
slight dip in the ground was screened by alders. No matter
how hot the day, a tremulous breath of coolness had always
touched their faces as they passed it. ... A child on a bicycle,
her teeth gleaming beneath a sun-hat – the sound of a bicycle
bell – a voice crying 'Look! I've taken my hands off!' ... In
those muddled memories was summed up all to which Thérèse
could cling. Mechanically, matching the words to the rhythm
of the horse's trot, she said over and over again to herself:
'The uselessness of my life: the emptiness of my life: unending

loneliness: no way out.' One gesture, and one only, would solve everything, but Bernard would never make it. If only he would take her in his arms and ask no questions! If only she could rest her head on a human shoulder, could weep knowing the comfort of a warm and human presence!

She saw the bank in the field on which, one blazing day, Jean Azévédo had sat. What a fool she was ever to have imagined that there might be some place in the world where she could sink to the earth with the knowledge that there were people round her who understood, who perhaps even admired and loved her! She was fated to carry loneliness about with her as a leper carries his scabs. 'No one can do anything for me: no one can do anything against me.'

'There's the Master and Miss Clara.'

Balion pulled on the reins. Two shadowy figures came forward. Bernard, though still very weak, was there to meet her – eager for reassurance. She half rose and, while they were still some distance off, cried out, 'Case dismissed!' All Bernard said was, 'I expected as much.' Then he helped his aunt into the trap and took the reins. Balion was left to walk back to the house. Aunt Clara sat between husband and wife. Thérèse had to shout in her ear that everything was settled (the poor old thing had only a very confused idea of what all the fuss had been about). As usual, she began to talk at breakneck speed. She said that *they* always did things in the same way: that it was the Dreyfus case all over again. 'Throw enough mud and some of it is bound to stick.' *They* were very powerful. The Republicans had been fools. They ought to have watched their step more closely. Give the beasts half a chance and they'd be on top of you. ... Her prattle made it unnecessary for the man and woman beside her to exchange a single word.

Aunt Clara, breathing heavily, climbed the stairs, a candle in her hand.

'Aren't you going to bed? Thérèse must be absolutely dead. You'll find a cup of soup in your room, and some cold chicken.'

But they remained standing in the hall. The old woman saw

Bernard open the drawing-room door, stand back to let Thérèse pass, and then follow her. If she had not been deaf she would have listened … but they didn't have to worry their heads about people like her who were buried alive. Nevertheless, she blew out her candle, crept downstairs again, and put her eye to the keyhole. Bernard was moving the lamp. His brightly lit face looked at once solemn and intimidated. She saw Thérèse's seated back. The young woman had thrown her coat and hat on to an arm-chair. Her wet shoes were steaming in front of the fire. For a moment she turned her face towards her husband, and the old woman rejoiced to see that she was smiling.

Thérèse was smiling. In the brief moment of time which had elapsed, the few yards of space which had intervened between house and stable, she, walking there at Bernard's side, had realized suddenly – or thought that she had realized – what it was that she must do. His mere approach had reduced to nothing any hope she might have had of explaining herself, of throwing herself on his mercy. How distorted in our minds the people we know best become when we are not actually with them! All through the journey she had been busy, quite unconsciously, creating a Bernard who might be capable of understanding, of trying to understand. But she had only to see him, even for a moment, to remember what he was really like – a man who had never once in his life put himself in another person's shoes, to whom the effort to get outside himself, to see himself as others saw him, was inconceivable. Would he, if it came to that, even listen? He strode up and down the damp, low-ceiled room. Here and there the wood-work of the floor was rotting. It creaked beneath his tread. Not once did he look at his wife. He was bursting with a desire to say all the things that he had long premeditated. She, too, knew what she was going to say. The simplest solution is always the one we never think of. She would say: 'I am going to vanish out of your life, Bernard. Don't bother your head any more about me. I will go into the night – now, at once, if you want me to. I am not frightened of the forest,

80

nor yet of the darkness. They know me: we know one another. I was created in the image of this barren land, where nothing lives but passing birds and the roaming wild boar. I accept your rejection of me. Burn all my photographs. Let my child grow up in ignorance even of my name. Let it be to the family as though I had never been.'

Already her lips were parted. She said:

'Let me just disappear, Bernard.'

At the sound of her voice he turned his head. He strode towards her out of the shadows. The veins of his forehead were swollen.

'What!' he sputtered, 'do you dare have an opinion? Are you brazen enough to express a wish? Don't say another word! Your business is to listen, to receive my orders – to abide by my irrevocable decision!'

He had got control of his voice now. He had carefully thought out what he was going to say, and now he was saying it. Leaning on the mantelpiece, he proceeded to express himself with portentous solemnity. He took a paper from his pocket and consulted it. Thérèse was no longer frightened: she wanted to laugh. He was just comic – a figure of fun. It did not matter what he said in that awful accent of his which everywhere but in Saint-Clair made him a laughing-stock – she was going away. Why all this fuss? It would not have made the slightest difference to anyone if this fool had disappeared from the face of the earth! The paper trembled in his hand, and she noticed his badly kept finger-nails. He was wearing no cuffs. He was just a country oaf who looked merely comic anywhere but in his accustomed rut, the kind of man who, from any intellectual, or even personal, point of view, is completely null and void. Only habit makes us attach importance to the life of the individual. Robespierre had been right – and Napoleon and Lenin. He noticed that she was smiling. The sight set him beside himself. He raised his voice. She *should* listen.

'I've got you where I want you – understand that! You will obey the decisions made by the family. If you don't ...'

'Well, if I don't – what?'

She no longer pretended to be indifferent. She faced him now with an air of mockery.

'Too late!' she cried: 'You gave evidence in my favour. You can't go back on what you said. If you do you will be guilty of perjury.'

'It is always possible to discover new facts. I've got one carefully locked away in my desk – proof positive that so far has not been made public. The law can't prevent me from producing *that*!'

She gave a start.

'What do you want me to do?' she asked.

He consulted his notes. For several seconds she was profoundly aware of the silence of Argelouse. Cockcrow was still far off. There was no sound of running water in this arid waste: no breeze stirred among the innumerable trees.

'I am not considering myself in this matter. For the moment I am out of the picture. The only thing I am worrying about is the family. Every decision of my life has been dictated by the interests of the family. For the honour of the family I consented to cheat justice. Let God be my Judge.'

His pomposity made Thérèse feel sick. She would have liked to tell him to say what he had to say more simply.

'For the sake of the family the world must suppose that we are in complete harmony. I shall make it quite clear that I believe in your innocence. On the other hand, I shall do everything in my power to protect myself. ...'

'Are you frightened of me, Bernard?'

In a low voice he said: 'Frightened? No: merely disgusted.' Then: 'I will come to the point and say what I have to say once and for all. Tomorrow we shall leave this place and move into the Desqueyroux house. It is not my wish that your aunt should live with us. Madame Balion will give you your meals in your room. You will be forbidden to enter any other, though you will be free to walk in the woods. On Sundays we shall attend High Mass at Saint-Clair together. You must be seen on my arm. On the first Thursday of each month we shall drive in an open carriage to the market at B—, and pay a visit to your father, as we have always done.'

'And Marie?'

'Marie will leave tomorrow with her nurse for Saint-Clair. Mother is going to take her to the South. We shall put it about that the state of her health has made change of air necessary. You didn't think, surely, that she was going to be left to *your* tender care? She, too, has got to be protected. Once I am dead and she has turned twenty-one, the property will go to her. First the husband, then the child. ... Why not?'

Thérèse got up. She wanted to scream.

'So you thought it was for the sake of your miserable trees that I ...'

Among all the myriad causes which had prompted her act this fool had not been able to understand a single one. He had had to invent the most squalid reason imaginable.

'Naturally – what other reason could there be? In matters like this one has to proceed by the method of elimination. I defy you to give me any other motive ... not that it is of the slightest importance. I am no longer interested in motives. You have ceased to have any meaning for me. The name you bear is the only thing that matters. In a few months' time, as soon as the fact of our reconciliation has been fully established, and Anne has married young Deguilheim ... you know, of course, that his parents have insisted on a delay ? they want to think things over ... in a few months' time, I say, I shall take up residence at Saint-Clair, and you will settle down here. We'll think up some plausible story – that you are suffering from neurasthenia, perhaps: something of that sort. ...'

'Wouldn't it do just to say that I am mad?'

'No, that would reflect on Marie. Don't worry; we'll find something.'

Thérèse murmured: 'Argelouse ... until I die. ...' She went over to the window and opened it. At this moment Bernard knew real happiness. Till now his wife had intimidated him, had made him feel small: but now *he* was on top! How conscious she must be of his contempt! His very moderation gave him a sense of pride. Madame de la Trave was never tired of telling him that he was a saint. The whole family

83

was loud in praise of his generous mind. For the first time he really felt that he was a great man. When, at the hospital, they had told him – oh, how tactfully! – of his wife's attempt upon his life, the calm way in which he had responded had earned him unstinted admiration – though it had cost him remarkably little effort. Nothing is ever wholly serious for those who are incapable of love. Because he was without love Bernard had felt only that flicker of joy which comes to a man when some great danger has been safely surmounted. He felt like a man who has just been told that for years, and in blissful ignorance, he has been living cheek by jowl with a dangerous lunatic. But this evening he was conscious of a new forcefulness. He felt that he was master of his fate. He realized, not without surprise, that nothing can resist the man of upright character who has a mind which can reason logically. Even though he had just come through a terrible ordeal, he was ready to maintain that no one is ever really unhappy save by his own fault. Nothing could be much worse than what he had experienced, yet he had settled it as he might have settled any other problem submitted to him for solution. Not that he would ever let it be generally known. He would save his self-respect. No one should pity him. He did not want pity. What was there so particularly humiliating in having married a monster? Nothing mattered so long as one had the last word. After all, there was a good deal to be said for the life of the unattached male. The close approach of death had put a marvellous edge on his appetite for possessions – on his taste for shooting, for driving his car, for eating and drinking – in short, for life!

Thérèse was still standing by the window. She could see a patch of white gravel, could smell the chrysanthemums growing there behind the fence which gave protection from the wandering cattle. Beyond the garden a dark mass of oaks hid the pines from view, but the scent of resin filled the darkness. They stood ranked there, like a hostile army, unseen but close at hand. She knew that the house was surrounded by them. Like muffled warders, moaning in the wind, they would watch her languish all the winter through, would hear

84

her gasp for breath in the stifling summer days. They would witness the slow process of her suffocation.

She closed the window, and turned back to Bernard.

'So you think you can keep me here by force?'

'I trust that you will make yourself quite at home. Only, please realize, once and for all, that if you leave this house it will be with handcuffs on your wrists.'

'Don't exaggerate! I know you too well to be bluffed, and there's no point in painting yourself blacker than you are. You would never expose the family to *that* disgrace. I'm not worrying.'

Like a man who has well weighed the pros and cons of a situation, he explained that by the very act of leaving she would tacitly admit her guilt. Should she choose to do so, then the family could avoid sharing in the general obloquy only by amputating the rotten limb, by casting her out, by publicly disclaiming her.

'That was what my mother, at first, wanted us to do. We were within an ace of letting justice take its course. Do you realize that? If it hadn't been for Anne and Marie ... But there is still time for us to change our minds. You needn't make your decision now. I give you until tomorrow.'

In a low voice Thérèse said:

'I've still got my father.'

'Your father sees eye to eye with us. He has his career to think about, his politics, the ideas for which he stands. He cares only about avoiding a scandal at all costs. You ought at least to show some gratitude for what he has done. If the prosecution broke down, it was entirely owing to him. ... I can scarcely believe that he has kept his decision from you.'

Bernard was no longer shouting. He had relapsed into a manner which was almost polite. It was not that he felt the slightest compassion. But this woman, whose breathing he could barely hear, was lying, at last, helpless at his feet. She was where she ought to be. The whole situation was getting itself very satisfactorily sorted out. Beneath such a blow any other man would have said good-bye to happiness. He took pride in the fact that he had managed to withstand the shattering shock. The world in general may be wrong: the world in general *had* been wrong about Thérèse – even Madame de la Trave, whose sharp eye for character had been bred of long practice. The trouble nowadays was that the world no longer set any value on moral principles, was no longer willing to admit that there may be great danger in the kind of education that Thérèse had received. No doubt she was a monster; still ... if only she had believed in God ... Fear is the beginning of wisdom.

So thought Bernard. He reflected that the small-town society, eager to taste the sweetness of the humiliation which had fallen on the Desqueyroux, would be nicely hoodwinked at the sight of so united a family each Sunday morning! He could hardly wait for Sunday to come round, so anxious was he to see his neighbours' faces! ... But Justice would not be cheated: he would see to that. ... He took the lamp and held it high so that the light fell on the back of Thérèse's neck.

'Are you coming up?'

She seemed not to hear him. He went out of the room, leaving her. Aunt Clara sat crouched on the bottom step of the stairs. She searched his face, and he smiled down at her with an effort. He took her arm, meaning to help her to her feet, but she resisted – like an old dog that will not stir from the bed-side of its dying master. Bernard set the lamp down on the tiled floor and shouted in her ear that Thérèse was already feeling better, but that she wanted to be left alone for a while before going to bed.

'You know that's one of her fads.'

Yes, her aunt knew it all right. It was always her misfortune to go into any room where Thérèse happened to be just when the young woman wanted to be alone. Often she had only to open a door the slightest little bit to realize that she was in the way.

She got up with an effort. Leaning on Bernard's arm, she reached her bedroom, which was immediately above the big drawing-room below. Bernard entered behind her in order to light the candle on her bed-table. Then he kissed her on the forehead and went out again. All this while her eyes had never left his face. She learned much from the features of those she could not hear. She waited until Bernard should have had time to reach his own room, then softly opened the door once more. But he was still on the landing, leaning against the banisters, rolling a cigarette. Hastily she withdrew, her knees trembling. So upset did she feel that she scarcely had sufficient strength left to undress.

She lay there on the bed, her eyes wide open.

10

DOWN in the drawing-room, Thérèse was sitting in the dark. A few embers still glowed red beneath the ashes. She did not move. From the depths of her memory, now that it was too late, rose scraps and fragments of the confession which she had prepared during her journey. But why reproach herself with having made no use of it? Truth to tell, the story which she had so carefully thought out, so neatly fitted together, had little connexion with reality. How stupid of her to have attached so much importance to what young Azévédo had said! No words of his had had the slightest influence on her. No; she had acted in obedience to some profound, some inexorable, law of her being. She had not brought destruction on this family: rather it was she who would be destroyed. They were right to look on her as a monster, but in her eyes they too were monstrous. They were planning slowly and surely to obliterate her, few thought the signs might be of their intention. 'From now on the whole powerful machinery of the family will be set in motion to crush me – unless, that is, I can either check its movement or slip, in time, from beneath its wheels. Useless to look for any other reason than that "they are they and I am I. ..." Less than two years ago I might have mustered strength enough to play the hypocrite, to save my face, to put them off the scent. There are others, I suppose (women in all respects like me), who could go on doing that until they died; women who might be saved by mere habit, drugged by custom, their senses deadened: women who might be content to sleep on in the bosom of the all-powerful family. But for me – for me, for me ...'

She got up, opened the window, and breathed in the chill dawn air. Why not escape? She had but to climb across the sill. Would they pursue her? Would they hand her over, once again, to justice? It was a chance worth taking. Anything would be better than this interminable agony. She dragged an arm-chair to the window, and set it firmly against the wall. But she had no money. Thousands of pine-trees might be hers in law, but without Bernard's agency she could not touch a single penny of her fortune. She would be no better off than Daguerre, the hunted murderer who had plunged at random into the heathy wastes. As a child she had been moved to pity for him (she remembered the policeman whom old Madame Balion had served with wine in the kitchen at Argelouse): it was the Desqueyroux dogs which had got on to the wretched man's scent. He had been found in the heather and brought back half dead with hunger. Thérèse had seen him lying trussed on a hay-cart. It was said that he had died on the boat before reaching Cayenne ... a boat, and then a prison cell. ... Weren't they perfectly capable of handing her over to the authorities as they had said they would do? What about the piece of evidence which Bernard pretended he had got up his sleeve? Probably it was all bluff ... unless, of course, he had found that packet of poison in the pocket of her old coat.

She *must* make certain. She began to feel her way up the stairs. The higher she climbed the more clearly could she see, because the dawn light was already paling the upper windows. On the attic landing stood a wardrobe which contained all the old clothes that were never given away because they came in useful during the shooting season. The faded old coat had a deep pocket. Aunt Clara used to stuff her knitting into it in those far-away days when she, too, had sat in a lonely cabin or 'jouquet', watching the flying duck.

Thérèse slipped her hand into it and brought out the little package sealed with wax:

Chloroform	..	..	..	.. 30 grams
Aconite drops	..	..	..	.. 20
Digitalin sol.	..	..	..	.. 20 grams

Once again she read the words, the figures. Death. She had always been terrified of dying. The important thing is not to look death squarely in the face – to see no farther than the immediately necessary actions – pouring out the water, dissolving the powder, gulping the stuff down, lying on the bed with her eyes closed. She mustn't try to look beyond those few simple motions. Why should she fear *that* sleep more than any other? She was shivering, but only because the early day struck cold. She went downstairs again and stopped outside the door of the room where Marie was sleeping. The nurse's snores were like the grunting of some animal. Thérèse pushed the door ajar. The waxing light was seeping through the shutters. The narrow iron bedstead showed white in the gloom. Two tiny fists lay on the coverlet. The still unformed profile lay sunk in the enfolding pillows. That over-large ear was *her* gift to the child. People were right. The form that lay unconscious there in sleep was a replica of herself. 'I am going away – but this part of myself will stay behind until it has fulfilled its destiny. Not a single iota will be omitted.' Tendencies, inclinations, laws of the blood – ineluctable laws. Somewhere Thérèse had seen accounts of desperate women who had taken their children with them to the grave. Decent folk, reading such things, would fling the paper from them. How could these things be? Being by nature a monster, Thérèse realized quite clearly that they very easily might be, and for next to no reason. ... Kneeling down, she touched one of the little hands very lightly with her lips. She was surprised to find that something from deep down in herself welled into her eyes and burned her cheeks: a few poor tears shed by one who never cried!

She got up, took one more look at the child, then went to her own room. She filled a glass with water, broke the wax on the little package, and hesitated, not knowing which of the boxes of poison she should choose.

The window was open. The cocks were tearing to shreds the morning mist which draped the branches of the pines with translucent tatters. The countryside lay soaked in dawn. How could she bring herself to abandon so much light? What is death? No one knows. Thérèse did not feel any certainty of annihilation. She could not be absolutely sure that nothing and Nobody awaited her. She loathed herself for feeling so much terror. Without a moment's thought she would have precipitated someone else into that nothingness, yet drew back when she herself stood there upon its verge. How humiliating cowardice can be! If that Being really did exist (for a brief moment she saw again that Corpus Christi day of blinding heat, a solitary man bowed down beneath a golden cope, the Something that he bore between his hands, his moving lips, his look of suffering) – since he *did* exist, let him prevent the criminal act while there was still time. Or, if it was his will that a poor blind soul should open for itself a way to death, let him at least receive with love the monster he had made. Thérèse poured the chloroform into the glass. Its name was familiar. It conjured up a picture of sleep, and so was the less terrifying. But she must hurry! The household was astir. Old Madame Balion had already thrown wide the shutters of Aunt Clara's room. What was it she was shouting into the deaf ears? She had grown used to making herself understood by the movement of her lips. There was a noise of opening doors and running feet. Thérèse had just time to throw a shawl over the table and so hide the poisons from sight. Madame Balion entered without knocking.

'Mademoiselle is dead! I found her fully dressed upon the bed – and already quite cold!'

Though the old lady had been an unbeliever, they put a rosary between her fingers and a crucifix upon her breast. Some of the local farmers came into the room, knelt, then left again – not without staring long and fixedly at Thérèse, who was standing at the bed's foot. ('For all we know, it may be her as done it.') Bernard went into Saint-Clair to break the news to the family and attend to the necessary business. He must have been thinking that this accident had fallen pat to the occasion, providing, as it did, diversion for the prying eyes.

Thérèse gazed at the body, the faithful old body which had lain down in front of her feet just as she was about to take her leap to death. Chance: coincidence. Had anyone spoken to her of a special intention, she would have shrugged her shoulders. People were saying to one another: 'Did you see her? – not even pretending to cry!' Deep in her heart Thérèse held colloquy with her who was no longer there. She would live on, but like a corpse at the mercy of those who hated her. She would try not to look beyond that fact.

At the funeral she occupied the place allotted to her. On the next Sunday she went to church with Bernard, who, instead of entering by a side-aisle as was his custom, made a point of walking down the nave for all to see. Thérèse kept her crape veil down until she had taken her seat between her husband and her mother-in-law. A pillar hid her from the congregation. There was nothing between her and the choir. On every other side she was hedged in. Behind her was the crowd of worshippers, on her right hand Bernard, Madame de la Trave on her left. Only in front of her was there a free and open space, empty as is the arena to the bull when he comes from the darkness into the light – space where, flanked by two small boys, a man in fancy dress was standing, his arms a little spread, whispering.

11

THAT same evening Bernard and Thérèse went back to Argelouse, to the Desqueyroux family house, which for years had hardly been lived in. The fires smoked, the windows were ill-fitting, and draughts came in under doors which the rats had gnawed. But so fine was the autumn this year that at first Thérèse did not suffer from these various inconveniences. Bernard was out with the guns until nightfall, and almost as soon as he got in he settled down in the kitchen, where he ate his evening meal with the Balions. Thérèse could hear the sound of forks, the drone of voices. In October it gets dark early. The small number of books which she had brought from the other house she knew from cover to cover. She asked Bernard to send an order to his bookseller in Bordeaux, but he did nothing about it, though he did allow her to renew her stock of cigarettes. ... There was little for her to do but poke the fire ... though the resinous smoke, blown down into the room, irritated her throat, which was already in a bad state from her over-indulgence in tobacco. Almost as soon as Madame Balion had cleared away the remains of her hasty meal she extinguished the lamp and went to bed. For hours she would lie, unvisited by sleep. The effect of the silence at Argelouse was to keep her awake. She liked best the nights when there was a high and gusty wind, for she seemed to find a hint of human tenderness in the monotonous soughing of the tree-tops. It lulled her, and when the equinox raged she slept better than in quiet and tranquil weather.

Interminable though the evenings were, she took to coming home before dusk – either because some farmer's wife, at sight of her, had caught her child by the hand and pulled it roughly within doors, or because a drover with whose name she had long been familiar had left her words of greeting unanswered. How lovely it would have been to lose, to drown, herself in a city crowd! At Argelouse every shepherd knew her story (even Aunt Clara's death was popularly laid to her charge). There was not a house that she dared enter. She had got into the way of leaving her home by a side-door, and she avoided the habitations of men. At the mere sound of an approaching cart she would hastily turn into a lane. She walked quickly, suffering in her heart the agonies of a hunted animal, and would lie in the heather to hide from a passing bicycle.

On Sundays, when she went into Saint-Clair for Mass, she was spared these terrors, and could enjoy a respite. The people of the little town seemed to be more kindly disposed. She did not know that her father and the de la Traves had represented her as a poor innocent, suffering under a mortal blow. 'We're terribly afraid that she'll never be herself again. She refuses to see anybody, and the doctor says that she must not be crossed. Bernard takes great care of her, but she seems to have lost the will to live. ...'

On the last night of October a wild wind from the Atlantic tossed the tormented tree-tops for hours together. In a half-sleep, Thérèse lay and listened to the thunder of the sea. But when she woke at dawn it was to a different sound. She opened the shutters, but the darkness of the room was unrelieved. A thin, dense rain was falling on the cobbles of the yard and pattering between the still thick foliage of the oaks. Bernard did not leave the house that day. Thérèse smoked, threw away her cigarette, went out on to the landing, and listened to him moving from room to room on the ground-floor. The smell of his pipe drifted up the stairs to her, overpowering the scent of her own much milder tobacco. The whole of her past life seemed to be concentrated in it. ... The first day of bad weather. ... What an endless vista of them lay before her, and through all that dreary time ahead she would just sit beside a dying fire doing nothing. The damp had loosened the paper in the corners of the room. She could see on the walls the marks left by the pictures which Bernard had taken for the drawing-room at Saint-Clair – and the rusty nails which no longer served any purpose at all. On the mantelpiece, in a triptych of artifical tortoiseshell, the photographs looked pale, as though the dead they pictured had died a second time: Bernard's father and grandmother, Bernard himself, dressed like one of the 'little Princes in the Tower'. Somehow or other she had got to get through the whole long day in that room, through weeks and months of such days. ...

When night came she could stand it no longer. Very quietly she opened the door, and went downstairs into the kitchen. She saw Bernard sitting in a low chair by the fire. At sight of her he jumped up. Balion stopped cleaning his gun. His wife let her knitting fall. So oddly did all three look at her that she said:

'Are you frightened of me?'

'You are forbidden to come into the kitchen – don't you know that?'

She made no answer, but backed towards the door. Bernard called her into the room.

'Since you're here, I may as well tell you that there is no longer any reason for my presence in this house. We have managed to create a sympathetic atmosphere in Saint-Clair. The people there believe, pretend to believe, that you are somewhat neurasthenic. It is generally understood that you prefer to live alone, and that I pay you frequent visits. From now on you need no longer go to Mass.'

She stammered back that she 'didn't at all mind going to Mass'. He replied that it wasn't a question of what she minded or didn't mind. The task they had set themselves had been accomplished.

'And since the Mass means nothing to you ...'

She opened her mouth, seemed about to say something, but remained silent. He saw to it that no word, no gesture, of hers should compromise this sudden and unexpected success. She asked how Marie was. He replied that she was in excellent health, and was leaving next day, with Anne and Madame de la Trave, for Beaulieu. He meant to join them there for a few weeks – a couple of months at most. He opened the door and stood back for her to pass.

In the darkness of the dawn she heard Balion putting in the horses, then the sound of Bernard's voice, the pawing of hooves, the bump and rattle of departing wheels, and, at last, when all was over, the pattering of rain upon the tiles and dirty windows, upon the empty fields and all the sixty miles of heath and bog, upon the shifting dunes and on the sea.

She lit another cigarette from the one she had just finished. About four o'clock she put on an oilskin and plunged into the rain. But the darkness frightened her and she went back to her room. The fire had gone out. She was shivering with cold, and went straight to bed. About seven Madame Balion brought her a fried egg on a rasher of ham, but she refused to eat it. The smell of fat made her feel sick. Never anything but *pâté* or ham. Madame Balion said that was the best she could do:

Monsieur Bernard had forbidden her to touch the poultry. She grumbled about being made to go up and down stairs to no purpose (she suffered from her heart, and had varicose veins). The work of the house was too much for her, she said. She had only consented to do it for Monsieur Bernard's sake.

That night Thérèse had a touch of fever. Her mind felt curiously clear, and in it she built up a complete picture of what life must be like in Paris. She saw again in imagination the restaurant in the Bois where she had once been in the old days – but now it was not Bernard who was with her, but Jean Azévédo and a crowd of young women. She put her tortoiseshell cigarette-case on the table and lit an Abdullah. She talked, baring her heart, while an orchestra played with muted strings. She held the circle of listening faces beneath her spell. Their owners were entranced, but not surprised. A woman said: 'Just like me – I've felt that way too.' A literary gentleman took her aside. 'You ought to write down your thoughts. We'll publish them in our magazine – the *Diary of a Modern Woman*.' A young man who was suffering torments for her sake drove her home in his car. They went up the Avenue du Bois. She was pleased rather than disturbed by the sense of all that unhappiness at her side. 'No,' she said; 'not to-night. I'm dining with a woman friend.' – 'What about to-morrow, then?' – 'No, not tomorrow, either.' – 'Are you never free in the evenings?' – 'Scarcely ever ... I might almost say never. ...'

Someone was in her life who made the rest of the world seem meaningless: someone completely unknown to the rest of her circle, someone very obscure and very humble. But her whole existence revolved about this sun which she alone could see, the heat of which she only could feel upon her flesh. Paris rumbled like the sound of the wind in the pines. The sensation of her companion's body pressed against her own, light though the contact was, hindered her breathing. But rather than push him away she would stop breathing altogether. (She made the gesture of pressing someone in her arms. She clasped her left shoulder with her right hand. The nails of her left hand dug into her right shoulder.)

She rose, barefooted, and opened the window. The night was far from cold, but somehow it was impossible to imagine that a day would ever come when it would not be raining. It would rain until the end of the world. If only she had money she would run away to Paris, would go straight to Jean Azévédo and throw herself on his mercy. He would manage to find her a job. How exquisite to be a woman alone in Paris, earning her own living, dependent on no one! ... To be without a family! ... to choose her friends as her heart dictated, prompted not by the tie of blood, but by the movement of the mind – and of the body too. How lovely to discover her own true kith and kin, no matter how widely scattered they might be. ... At last she went to sleep, leaving the window open. She awoke to a cold, wet dawn. Her teeth were chattering. She could not bring herself to get up and close the window. She was incapable even of stretching out her arm and pulling up the coverlet.

That day she did not get up at all, did not even tidy herself. She swallowed a few mouthfuls of *pâté* and some coffee, just in order that she might be able to smoke (tobacco on an empty stomach made her ill). She strove to recapture her fantasies of the previous night. There was scarcely more noise in Argelouse than there had been then, and the gloom of the afternoon was almost nocturnal. On these, the shortest days of the year, the solidly falling rain made all time seem as one. There was nothing to separate the hours. One dusk joined hands with another. It existed, as it were, in a motionless medium of silence. But she had no desire to sleep. Her dreams took on a sharper precision of outline. She sought deliberately in her past for facts long since forgotten, for lips that from afar she had adored, for bodies vaguely recognized which chance meetings and the random happenings of dream had brought into innocent contact with her own. She composed a symphony of happiness, invented a world of delights, built up from odds and ends a wholly impossible universe of love.

'She's not even bothering to get up now – leaves the *pâté* and the bread untasted,' said Madame Balion to her husband.

'But I'll take my oath she drinks the bottle dry. She'd get through as much liquor as one cared to give her, the slut! – and when she's had her fill, she burns the sheets with cigarette ends. She'll finish by setting the house on fire. She smokes so much that her fingers and nails are as yellow as though they'd been soaked in arnica. It's a wicked shame – them sheets as was woven on the place. ... Well, she won't get any clean ones out of me!'

It wasn't she – so the complaint went on – who refused to sweep the room or make the bed. But what could she do if that lazy-bones never got up? Why should she toil up and down stairs with jugs of hot water, and her with varicose veins and all? There they'd be at night, standing just where she'd put them in the morning.

Thérèse's mind drifted away from the unknown body of flesh and blood which she had conjured up for her delight. She grew weary of her happiness, felt the satiety of her imagined pleasures – and invented new methods of escape. People (she pretended) were kneeling round her truckle bed. A child from Argelouse (one of those who commonly fled at her approach) was brought dying to her room. She touched it with her hand – all yellowed with nicotine – and it got up, cured. Other, humbler, dreams, she improvised – seeing, in imagination, a house at the sea's edge, a garden, and a terrace. She set about arranging the rooms, choosing the furniture piece by piece, deciding where to put what she had brought from Saint-Clair, involving herself in long arguments about covers and materials. Then the scene would fade, losing its clearness of outline, until nothing remained but a beech-hedge and a bench overlooking the sea. Seated there, she rested her head on her companion's shoulder, rose at the sound of the dinner-gong, entered the gloom of the long pleached alley. Someone walking at her side put sudden arms about her, held her close. A kiss, she thought, can stay the wheel of time. The seconds of love can draw out to infinity. Or so she imagined, for she would never know. She saw the house, still gleaming white, the well. Somewhere a pump creaked. Freshly watered heliotrope scented the air. Dinner would be an interval of rest before the evening's happiness, before that night of which she could not think, so far did it exceed the power of human heart to contemplate. Thus did the love of which, more than any living creature, she had been deprived, possess and penetrate her utterly. She scarcely heard old Madame Balion's complaints. What was the woman saying? That Monsieur Bernard would come back from the south one of these days without warning. 'And what'll he say when he sees this room looking like a pigsty?' If Madame wouldn't get up of her own accord, she'd have to be made to. Seated upon the bed, Thérèse was horrified by the sight of her skinny legs. The feet looked, to her eyes, enormous. Madame Balion wrapped her in a dressing-gown and pushed her into a chair. She felt beside her for her cigarettes, but her hand met only emptiness. A cold shaft of sunlight entered through the window. Madame Balion fussed about with a broom, short of breath, wheezing and grumbling – yet, for all that, she was a good soul, for it was common knowledge that at Christmas-time she cried when her fattened pig was killed. She resented Thérèse's silence, regarding it as an insult, as a sign of contempt.

But it was not for Thérèse to decide whether she should speak or not. When her body felt the coolness of clean sheets she thought she had said 'Thank you,' when, in fact, no sound had issued from her lips.

Madame Balion, at the door, threw back at her: 'Well, you won't burn those!' Thérèse, terrified lest she had taken the cigarettes, stretched her hand to the table. The cigarettes were no longer there. How could she live without smoking? Her fingers *must* be able continually to know the feel of that tiny object, so dry, so warm. She must have the smell of tobacco in her nostrils: the room must be filled with the thin vapour which she inhaled and then breathed out. Madame Balion would not come near her till the evening. A whole afternoon without tobacco! She closed her eyes. Her stained fingers made the accustomed gesture of holding a cigarette.

At seven o'clock Madame Balion came into the room with a candle, and set a tray upon the table: milk, coffee, a scrap of bread. 'Anything else you want?' She waited malevolently for

Thérèse to ask for cigarettes. But Thérèse still lay with her face to the wall, and did not turn her head.

Madame Balion must have neglected to fasten the window. A gust of wind blew it open, and the chill night air filled the room. Thérèse could not muster sufficient energy to throw back the bedclothes, to get up and cross the room on bare feet to shut it. She lay curled in the bed, the sheet drawn half-way over her face, so that only on her eyes and forehead did she feel the icy blast. The deep murmur of the pines filled Argelouse, but, despite this sound, as of a fretting sea, the silence of the place was there. If she were really in love with suffering (she thought) she would not lie huddled thus beneath the bedclothes. She tried to throw them off a little, but could not long endure the cold. She tried again, and this time succeeded in remaining a longer while uncovered. It was as though she were playing a game with herself. Almost without her willing it, her pain had become her sole preoccupation, the sole reason – why not? – of her existence.

12

'A LETTER from Monsieur.'

Because Thérèse did not take the envelope which Madame Balion held out the old servant began to nag her. Monsieur, no doubt, had written to say when he would be coming back. She must know, so as to have everything ready.

'Would Madame rather that I read it to her?' 'All right, read it!' Thérèse said: and then, as always, when Madame Balion was in the room, turned her face to the wall. But the words that the voice spelled out roused her from her apathy.

'I was glad to hear from Balion that all goes well at Argelouse. ...'

Bernard wrote that he was coming home by road. Since, however, he intended to stay at several towns on the way, he could not say exactly when he would arrive.

'... It certainly won't be later than 20 December. Don't be surprised when you see Anne and the Deguilheim boy with me. They got engaged at Beaulieu, but it's not yet official. He particularly wants to see you first. Merely a matter of good manners, he says, but I have a feeling that he wants to make up his mind about you know what. You are far too intelligent not to get through the ordeal with flying colours. Remember that you are a very sick woman, and a nervous wreck. I rely on you. Perhaps I may show my gratitude to you for not spoiling Anne's happiness or in any way compromising the successful issue of a scheme which, in every way, is so satisfactory for the family. But if anything goes wrong, if you try to sabotage the arrangement, I can make you pay dearly. I shouldn't have the slightest scruple about doing so. But I feel quite certain that nothing of the kind would occur to you.'

The day was fine and bright, though cold. Obedient to Madame Balion's instructions, Thérèse got up and went for a short walk in the garden, leaning on her arm. But she had great difficulty in finishing her wing of chicken. There were still ten days to go before 20 December. If only Madame would make a little effort. Ten days were more than enough time in which to get her up and about again.

'No one could say she's not trying,' said Madame Balion to her husband. 'She's doing what she can. Monsieur Bernard's a great hand at training vicious dogs. You've seen him at it, with that special collar of his. It didn't take him long to get our fine lady upstairs crouching and whimpering. But he'd be wise not to count his chickens ...'

Thérèse, in fact, was doing everything possible to free herself from her dream fantasies, to fight her way back from sleep and nothingness. She forced herself to walk and eat, but especially to recapture her clearness of vision, to see things and people with her bodily eyes. And since the waste land to which now she came had been fired by her own hand, since she must tread on still warm ashes, and find her way through burned and blackened trees, she would do her best to talk and smile in the bosom of the family – his family.

On the 18th, at about three o'clock of an overcast but rain-less day, she was seated in front of the fire in her room, leaning back in her chair with her eyes closed. The purring of a motor-car awoke her. She heard Bernard's voice in the hall, and Madame de la Trave's as well. When Madame Balion, panting and breathless, opened the door without knocking, she was already on her feet before the glass, putting rouge upon her lips and cheeks. She said: 'I mustn't frighten the poor young man.' But Bernard, in not going straight up to see his wife, blundered. Young Deguilheim, who had promised his family to 'keep his eyes skinned', said to himself that 'at the very least it showed a lack of eagerness and made one think'. He moved a pace or two away from Anne and turned up the fur collar of his coat, remarking that 'it's never any good trying to warm these country rooms'. He addressed himself to Bernard: 'I suppose you've got no cellar? Without a cellar you're bound to get dry-rot in the floors, unless you have them laid on cement. ...'

Anne de la Trave was wearing an overcoat of light grey cloth and a felt hat without ribbon or trimming of any sort ('though,' said Madame de la Trave, 'it costs more like that than the hats we used to have with all those feathers and aigrettes. But, of course, it's the very finest quality felt from Lailhaca's – a Reboux model.') Madame de la Trave stretched her feet to the fire. Her face, at once imperious and puffy, was turned towards the door. She had promised Bernard not to let him down. But she had warned him that he must not ask her to kiss his wife. 'You wouldn't I'm sure, expect your mother to do any such thing. It'll be bad enough having to take her hand. God knows, she was sufficiently guilty, but that's not what I mind most. There have always been people capable of murder – we all know that ... it's her hypocrisy that I can't forgive! That's what really shocks me. Do you remember how she used to say, "Take this arm-chair, Mother, you'll be more comfortable"? ... And then, how nervous she always pretended to be about frightening you. ... "The poor darling is so terrified of dying: the very idea of going to see a doctor might be fatal. ..." God knows, I never had the faintest suspicion, but I confess that "poor darling" on her lips *did* somewhat surprise me.'

Now, in the Argelouse drawing-room, she was conscious

only of the general atmosphere of embarrassment. She noticed young Deguilheim's little bird-like eyes fixed on Bernard.

'Bernard, you really ought to go and see what Thérèse is doing. ... She may be feeling worse.'

Anne (indifferent, and seemingly not interested in what might happen next) was the first to recognize a familiar step. 'I can hear her coming downstairs.' Bernard, his hand pressed to his heart, was suffering from an attack of palpitations. He was a fool not to have arrived the previous night. He ought to have arranged with Thérèse all the details of this meeting. What was she going to say? He wouldn't put it beyond her to spoil everything, though without committing herself to anything sufficiently definite to be held against her. How slowly she was coming downstairs! When, at last, she opened the door, they were all on their feet, looking in her direction.

Bernard was to remember, many years later, that, as this woman with the wasted body and the small, white, painted face came into the room, his first thought had been 'The Dock'. But it was not because of her crime that the words had come into his mind. In a flash he saw again the coloured picture torn from the *Petit Parisien* which, with many others, had adorned the wooden outside lavatory in the garden at Argelouse; and how, on a blazing hot day, while the flies buzzed and the grasshoppers were noisy in the fields, his childish eyes had gazed at the red and green daub representing the *Woman Prisoner of Poitiers*. With just such eyes he gazed now at Thérèse, a bloodless figure, little more than skin and bone. He realized what a fool he had been not, at any cost, to have kept that terrible figure out of sight. He ought to have got rid of her, as one gets rid of an infernal machine – by throwing it into the water before it can explode. Whether intentionally or not, Thérèse had brought into the room an atmosphere of drama – worse still, of newspaper gossip. One of two things she must be – either criminal or victim. ... There broke from the family a murmur of astonishment. and pity. So little feigned was it that young Deguilheim hesitated to draw any conclusion. He no longer knew what to think.

Thérèse said: 'There's nothing to worry about. The bad weather has been keeping me indoors, and I have lost my appetite. I've been eating hardly anything. But I'd rather get thin than fat. ... Anne, dear, let us talk of your affairs. I am so happy ...'

She took the girl's hands (she was seated, Anne still standing), and looked at her. In the face now worn to a skeleton thinness Anne recognized the old intense look which once she had found so irritating. She remembered how she used to say: 'When you've quite finished looking at me like that!'

'I rejoice in your happiness, Anne dear. ...' She directed a brief smile at the cause of 'Anne's happiness', at young Deguilheim, with his receding hair, his policeman's moustache, and his drooping shoulders. She took in the short coat he was wearing, the fat little legs in their grey and black striped trousers. (What was there so surprising about him – he was just another man, just a husband.) Then her eyes went back to Anne, and she said:

'Take off your hat. ... Ah! now I know it's you, darling!'

Anne saw close to her a faintly grimacing mouth and a pair of dry, tearless eyes. But she did not know what Thérèse was thinking. The Deguilheim boy was saying that winter in the country was not so bad for a woman who is fond of her home. 'There's always so much to do in a house.'

'Don't you want to hear about Marie?'

'Yes, yes, of course I do. ... Tell me about her.'

Anne seemed to have got back into her old mood of hostility and mistrust. For months she had been saying, in a voice that held just her mother's inflexions: 'I'd overlook almost anything, because, after all, she really is terribly ill, but I just can't bear the way she shows no interest whatever in her child. I think it's absolutely beastly of her!' Thérèse could read the girl's thoughts. 'She's holding it against me that I wasn't the one to start talking about Marie. How *can* I explain it all to her? She'd never understand that my mind is filled with my own concerns, that nobody interests me but myself. She lives for the day when she has children of her own in whom she can become completely lost and absorbed. In that way she's just like her mother – and all the other women of her family. But with me it's different. I've always got to be the centre of my own picture; I *must* get myself in focus. ... My little scrap of misery has only got to start whining, for Anne to forget all about the odd tension which was always between her and me when we were girls, all about Jean Azévédo's kisses ... she flies straight to the child without waiting even to take her coat off. The women of her family are all the same. They ask nothing better than to lose themselves in something or some-one else. Such complete surrender to the interests of the species, such utter self-effacement and annihilation, is very beautiful, of course ... but, somehow, it's not for me. ...'

She tried not to listen to what the others were saying, to concentrate her thoughts wholly on Marie. Very soon now the child would be beginning to talk. 'It'll amuse me to hear her for a moment or two, but I shall very soon get bored, and all impatient to be alone with myself again.'

Turning to Anne, she said: 'She's really beginning to talk quite well, isn't she?'

'She can repeat anything one says – it's really terribly funny. ...'

Thérèse thought: 'I *must* listen to what they're saying. My mind's a complete blank. What's the Deguilheim boy talking about?' She strained her ears, trying to catch the words.

'The men on my Balisac property don't do half the work on the trees that yours do. The chaps here get twice the yield of resin. ...'

'Yours must be bone-idle, then, with the stuff fetching the price it does. ...'

'Do you realize that at the present time a man cutting for resin can make as much as a hundred francs a day? ... But I'm afraid we're tiring your wife. ...'

Thérèse leaned back in her chair. Everyone got up. Bernard decided not to go back to Saint-Clair. Young Deguilheim fell in with the suggestion that he should drive the car. The chauffeur could bring it back next day with Bernard's things. Thérèse made an effort to get up, but her mother-in-law laid a restraining hand on her.

She closed her eyes. She heard Bernard say to Madame de la Trave: 'Really, that Balion couple! I'm going to give them a piece of my mind! ...' – 'Be careful what you say, it might be awkward if they gave notice. They know too much ... besides, I really don't see how you'd get on without them. ... No one knows the details of the estate as Balion does.'

Bernard said something which Thérèse did not catch, but she heard Madame de la Trave's reply: 'All the same, don't be rash ... and whatever happens, be sure not to trust *her*. You must watch her every movement, and never let her go into the kitchen or the dining-room alone. ... Don't worry; she's not fainted. She's asleep, or pretending to be.'

Thérèse opened her eyes. Bernard was standing in front of her. There was a glass in his hand. He said: 'Drink this – it's Spanish wine: it'll do you good.' And because he always did what he had a mind to do, he proceeded to work himself up into a fury, and stormed into the kitchen. Thérèse could hear voices raised in a babble of brogue. She thought: 'He was obviously afraid of something – but of what?' He came back.

'I think you'd eat with a better appetite in the dining-room than upstairs. I've given orders for your place to be laid as it always used to be.'

He was once more as he had been during the trial – her ally, intent, at all costs, on getting her out of a mess. He had made up his mind that she must get well again. It was plain that something had given him a fright. Thérèse watched him sitting opposite her, poking the fire. But she could not see into his mind, could not guess that what those large eyes saw in the flames was the red-and-green picture from the *Petit Parisien – The Woman Prisoner of Poitiers*.

In spite of all the rain that had fallen there were no puddles in the sandy soil of Argelouse. Even in the depths of winter one hour of sunshine was enough to dry the ground sufficiently to make it possible to walk without discomfort in rope-soled sandals over the dry, springy carpet of needles which overlay the roads. Bernard was out all day, shooting, but came home to meals. He was worried about Thérèse, and looked after her as he had never done before. Relations between them had become fairly easy. He made her weigh herself every three days, and cut down her smoking to two cigarettes after each meal. On his advice, she did a lot of walking. 'Exercise is the best way of getting an appetite.' She was no longer afraid of Argelouse. It seemed to her that the wall of pine-trees had withdrawn and grown less dense: as though they were pointing out to her a way of escape. One evening Bernard said: 'All I ask is that you should wait until Anne is safely married. The neighbours must see us, just once more, together. As soon as the ceremony is over you can do as you like.' That night she had been unable to sleep. An uneasy happiness made it impossible for her to close her eyes. At dawn she heard the clamour of innumerable cocks. She got the impression that they were not so much answering one another as all crowing at the same moment, filling earth and sky with their noise. Bernard would turn her loose upon the world as he had turned the old sow which he had never succeeded in domesticating loose upon the heath. Once Anne was married people could say what they liked. He would drop Thérèse into the unplumbable depths of Paris and then take to his heels. Everything was arranged between them. There would be no divorce, no legal separation. Some excuse about her health could be trumped up to satisfy the world at large ('she's never really well unless she's travelling'). Each November he would see that she got her fair share of the profits from her resin.

He asked no questions about her plans: she could go hang herself for all he cared – provided it wasn't at Argelouse. 'I shan't know a quiet moment,' he said to his mother, 'until she's out of the way.' – 'I suppose she'll resume her maiden name, but that won't prevent people from putting two and two together if she gets up to her old tricks again.' But Thérèse, he insisted, kicked only when she was between shafts. Left to herself, she might be more sensible. In any case, that was a risk they'd got to take. In this opinion Monsieur Larroque fully concurred. All things considered, the best thing would be for Thérèse to disappear altogether. Like that, she would be soon forgotten. People would quickly get out of the way of talking about her. The important thing was that the whole wretched business should be buried in silence. This idea had taken such deep root in their minds that nothing could shift it. Thérèse must be got from between the shafts. How impatient they were to have it all over and done with!

She loved the way in which the tail-end of winter stripped the bare earth and made it barer still, though even then the dead leaves clung tenaciously to the oaks. She discovered that what she had always thought of as the silence of Argelouse had no real existence. On the quietest day there was a murmur in the forest, as though the trees were gently crying themselves to sleep, moaning a muted lullaby which turned the nights into a time of ceaseless whispering. In the days to come there were to be many hopeless dawns, though at present she could not imagine such a possibility – dawns so empty that they would make her look back with regret to those wakeful hours at Argelouse when only the clamour of the farmyard filled the silence. She was to remember, in those future summers, the grasshoppers by day and, at night, the crickets. In Paris, she was to know, not blasted and tormented pines, but the terror of men and women: a crowd of persons after a crowd of trees.

Husband and wife grew astonished to find so little awkwardness between them. We find our fellow-creatures tolerable, thought Thérèse, once we know that it is in our power to leave them. Bernard took a lively interest in her weight, but also in her words. She spoke to him now more freely than she had ever done before. 'In Paris – when I'm settled in Paris ...' She would live in an hotel and, perhaps, look round for a flat. She was planning to attend courses, lectures, concerts. She meant to start her education over again 'from the beginning'. It never occurred to Bernard to watch her movements. He ate his food and drank his wine without any sign of hesitation. Dr Pédemay, who often met them on the road to Argelouse, said to his wife: 'What makes it all so odd is that they don't seem to be shamming.'

13

AT about ten o'clock of a warm March morning the human tide was already flowing strongly. It lapped at the terrace of the Café de la Paix in front of which Bernard and Thérèse were seated. She dropped her cigarette and – sign that she was a true daughter of the heathlands – carefully put her foot on it.

'Afraid of setting fire to the pavement, eh?' Bernard laughed, but it was only with something of an effort that he did so. He blamed himself for having come with her as far as Paris. He had done so partly because, with Anne's marriage only just past, he was anxious not to give the neighbours any cause for gossip, but also because she had wanted him to. She had, he told himself, a genius for putting one in a false position. So long as she remained part of his life there would always be the risk of his making these irrational gestures. Even on a nature as solid and as well-balanced as his own this wild creature still, to some extent, exercised an influence. Now, at the moment of parting, he could not but feel a pang of melancholy ill-suited though it was to his general mood. It was utterly unlike him to have any such feeling, to submit thus to the impact of another person (especially when that other person was Thérèse: he would never have imagined it to be possible). How impatient he was to cut free of the whole sorry business! He would not know a moment's peace until he was safely seated in the train which left at noon. The car would be waiting for him that evening at Langon. Very soon after leaving the station at Villandraut the pines begin. He looked at Thérèse's profile as she sat there beside him, staring at her as he would so often stare at some face seen in a crowd, watching it until it vanished.

Suddenly:

'Thérèse,' he said, 'there's just one thing I want to ask you ...' He averted his eyes. He had never been able to endure her fixed gaze. Hastily he finished the sentence: 'Was it because you hated me – because you had a horror of me?'

His own words filled him with an emotion of astonishment and irritation. Thérèse smiled, but when she turned to look at him her face was serious again. Bernard had actually asked her a question – and the very question she herself would have asked had she been in his position. The confession so long pondered and prepared as she drove in the Victoria along the Nizan road, and, later, in the local train to Saint-Clair, on that night of queries and patient self-examination when she had tried so hard to trace the act back to its source, only to exhaust herself in a frenzy of introspection – that experience was at last, then, to have its reward. Unknown to herself she had troubled Bernard's peace of mind. She had tangled him in a maze of uncertainty, so that he had been forced to question her, like a man who cannot see his way clear before him, but gropes and hesitates. He was no longer the simple creature he had been: consequently, he was no longer implacable. Upon the stranger at her side Thérèse fixed a sympathetic, almost a maternal, gaze. But her answer, when it came, was mocking.

'Do you mean to say you don't realize that it was for the sake of your trees? ... I wanted, you see, to have sole possession of them.'

He shrugged his shoulders.

'I don't believe that now – if I ever did. What *was* your motive? You can be perfectly frank with me – now.'

She stared before her into space. On this pavement, this bank above a river of mud and humanity into which she was about to plunge, knowing that she must fight to keep her head above water if she were not to be sucked down into the depths, she saw a gleam of light, a hint of dawn. She played in imagination with the idea of going back to the sad and secret land – of spending a lifetime of meditation and self-discipline in the silence of Argelouse, there to set forth on the great adventure of the human soul, the search for God. ... A Moroccan with carpets and strings of beads for sale, thinking she was smiling at him, approached. On the same note of mockery she said:

'I was about to say that I don't really know why I did it. But now at last I believe that I do! I'm not sure that it wasn't simply to see that look of uncertainty, of curiosity – of unease which, a moment ago, I caught in your eyes!'

He started to rate her in a way that brought back memories of their honeymoon:

'Still talking for effect! – up to the very last moment! ... Do, for Heaven's sake, be serious. Why was it?'

She was no longer laughing, but, in her turn, asked a question:

'You're the kind of man, aren't you, Bernard, who always knows precisely why he does a thing?'

'Naturally ... at least, I think I do.'

'I should like nothing better than to make the whole thing crystal-clear to you. You've no idea how I have tortured myself in an effort to see straight. But if I did give you a reason it would seem untrue the moment I got it into words. ...'

He was becoming impatient:

'But there must have been some stage at which you made up your mind, at which you took the first step?'

'There was – it was on the day of the great fire at Mano.'

They had suddenly achieved intimacy, and were speaking now in low voices. Here, in this busy Paris street, with a mild sun shining and a rather chilly wind blowing, smelling of American tobacco and agitating the red and yellow awnings, she found it odd to conjure up the picture of that oppressive afternoon with its pall of smoke through which the blue looked dimmed and sooty, to smell again the acrid scent as of torches which comes from burning pines. In her drowsed and brooding mind she thought of a crime slowly taking shape.

'It really all began in the dining-room. There was not much light – there never was at midday. You had your head turned towards Balion, and were busy talking: so busy that you never thought to count the drops falling into your glass.'

So intent was she on not omitting a single detail of her story that she did not look at him. But she heard him laugh, and the sound brought back her eyes to his face. Yes, he was actually laughing, in the same stupid way with which she had once been so familiar. He said: 'Come now, what do you take me for?' Obviously, he didn't believe her. (Who would have, if it came to that?) He continued to chuckle, and she recognized the old Bernard, the Bernard who had always been sure of himself, who had never let anyone get the better of him. He was once more securely in the saddle. Suddenly she felt lost and helpless. He began to tease her.

'So the idea came to you quite on the spur of the moment, did it? – almost like a visitation of Grace?'

How he hated himself for ever having questioned her! By so doing he had lost the advantage of that attitude of contempt by which he had dominated her mad, unbalanced moods. She was actually getting the bit between her teeth again! Why had he ever given way to that sudden desire to understand? – as though with women of her irresponsible type there was ever anything *to* understand! But impulse had got the better of him. He had not stopped to think. ...

'I'm not telling you all this, Bernard, in order that you should think me innocent – quite the contrary!'

She went on to accuse herself with a strange urgency. She could only – she made it clear – have acted in that half-mechanical, that somnambulistic fashion, because for months past she had not attempted to resist, had, indeed, been encouraging, criminal thoughts. Once the first step had been taken, with what devilish clear-sightedness, with what tenacity, had she carried through her scheme!

'I never felt that I was being cruel – except when my hand hesitated. I detested myself for prolonging your sufferings. I felt that I must get the whole thing over and done with as quickly as possible. I was the victim of a terrible duty. Yes, honestly, I had the feeling that it was a duty.'

Bernard broke in on her:

'Talk, talk, talk! For Heaven's sake, do try, once and for all, to tell me what it was you wanted! The truth of the matter is, you can't!'

'What I wanted? It would be a great deal easier to tell you what I didn't want. I didn't want to be for ever playing a part, to go through a series of movements, to continue speaking words, that were not my own: in short, to deny at every moment of the day a Thérèse who ... Oh, Bernard, my one wish is to be absolutely truthful about all this. Why does every word I utter sound so *sham*?'

'Speak lower; the man in front just looked round.'

By this time he had only one desire – to put an end to their discussion. But he knew her wild moods only too well. Nothing would please her better than to go on splitting hairs. She, too, realized that the man beside her, with whom she had been caught up in a moment's intimacy, had once more become a stranger. But she forced herself to go on, tried on him the effect of her most charming smile, spoke in the low, hoarse tones that once he had loved.

'But I know now, Bernard, that the Thérèse who instinctively stamps out a cigarette because the tiniest spark will set heather on fire – the Thérèse who used to love counting over her tale of pines and reckoning her profits – the Thérèse who took pride in marrying a Desqueyroux and so becoming one of a good county family, in settling down, as they say – I know now that *that* Thérèse is just as real, just as much alive, as the other. There was no good reason why she should be sacrificed to the other.'

'What other do you mean?'

She did not know what answer to make. He looked at his watch. She said:

'I shall have to come down from time to time on business – and to see Marie.'

'What business? *I* look after our joint property: we've had all that out. Why bring it up again? You will, of course, be included in all official ceremonies at which it is important, for the honour of our name and in Marie's interest, that we be seen together. In a family as large as ours there is never, thank goodness, any lack of weddings – or of funerals either, if it comes to that. Which reminds me, I should be very much surprised if Uncle Martin lasted out the summer. ... That'll give you an opportunity, since, seemingly, you've already ...'

A mounted policeman put a whistle to his lips, swung open an invisible pair of lock-gates, and a flood of pedestrians surged across the black roadway before it should be submerged by the oncoming tide of taxis. 'I ought to have slipped away one night and made for the southern part of the heath, like Daguerre. I ought to have walked through the sickly pine clumps of that barren land – walked until I could walk no longer. I should never have had the courage to put my head in a pond and keep it there (like that Argelouse shepherd did last year because his daughter-in-law wouldn't give him enough to eat). But I could, at least, have slept on the sandy soil and closed my eyes – though there are crows, of course, and ants, who don't wait until ...'

She looked at the human flood, the mass of living and breathing humanity, which was about to open before her, roll over her, envelop her. There was nothing more she could do. Bernard took out his watch again.

'Quarter to eleven ... Just time to look in at the hotel. ...'

'Won't you be too hot on the journey?'

'I must have something extra to put on this evening in the car.'

She saw in imagination the road along which he would drive, could almost feel the cold wind on her face, the wind smelling of marsh and pine-clad slopes, of mint and country mists. She looked at him with that smile upon her lips which once had made old countrywomen: say 'No one could say she's pretty, but she's a bit of living charm.' Had Bernard said, 'All is forgiven; come back with me,' she would have got up there and then and followed him. But Bernard was annoyed to think that he had given way to a moment's sentiment, was filled with distaste at the thought of going through unaccustomed movements and using the words that were not the words of every day. He 'fitted' the well-trodden roads of life, as his carts fitted the lanes of their home country. He needed the clearly marked ruts. Once let him get back into them, as he would have done when he sat this evening in the dining-room at Saint-Clair, and the peace and calm of habitual things would be his again.

'For the last time, Bernard, I want to say how terribly sorry I am. ...'

She made the words sound a little too solemn, a little too hopeless – it was her final effort to keep their conversation going. But all she got from him was a protest: 'Oh, please don't let us go into all that again.'

'You'll feel very lonely. Even though I shan't be in the house I shall still be in your life. It would be much better for you if I were dead.'

He just perceptibly shrugged. In a tone that was almost gay, he begged her 'not to worry about him'.

'Every generation of Desqueyroux has had its old bachelor, and that is what I ought to have been. I have all the necessary qualities for the part (you can't deny that, can you?). My one regret is that our child was a girl, because it means that the name will die out. Though, of course, even if we had stayed together, we shouldn't have wanted another ... so, on the whole, all's well that ends well. ... Don't bother to come with me; just stay on here.'

He hailed a taxi, and turned his head as he was getting into it to tell her that he had paid for their drinks.

For a long time she sat staring at the drop of port in the bottom of Bernard's glass; then, once more, gave her whole attention to the passers-by. Some of them seemed to be waiting, walking up and down the pavement. There was a woman who twice turned and smiled at her (a working-girl, or someone got up to look like a working-girl?). It was the hour of the day at which the dressmakers' workrooms empty. Thérèse had no intention of leaving. She felt neither bored nor sad. She decided that she would not pay Jean Azévédo a visit that afternoon – and heaved a sigh of relief. She did not want to see him, to embark on another conversation, another endless effort to find the right words. She knew Jean Azévédo, but the kind of people she wanted to meet she did not know. Of one thing only was she certain, that they would not call on her for words. No longer did she feel afraid of loneliness. It was enough that she need not move. Had she been lying on the heathland to the south, her body would have been a magnet for ants and dogs. Here, too, she felt herself already at the heart of an obscure ebb and flow. She was hungry. She got up. In the window of the *Old England* tea-shop she saw herself reflected, and realized how young she was. The close-fitting travelling suit became her well. But those years at Argelouse had left their mark upon her face. She looked worn and haggard. She took note of her short nose and too prominent cheek-bones. 'I'm not an old woman yet', she thought. She lunched (as so often in her dreams) in the rue Royale. Why go back to the hotel? She had no wish to. The half-bottle of Pouilly she had drunk filled her with a warm sense of well-being. She asked for some cigarettes. A young man at the next table snapped his lighter and held it out to her. She smiled. Difficult to believe that only an hour ago she had been longing to drive with Bernard along the road to Villandraut in the evening light between the ominous pines! What did it matter – the sort of country one was fond of, pines or maples, sea or plain? Life alone was interesting, people of flesh and blood. 'It is not the bricks and mortar that I love, nor even the lectures and museums, but the living human forest that fills the streets, the creatures torn by passions more violent than any storm. The moaning of the pines at Argelouse in the darkness of the night thrilled me only because it had an almost human sound!'

She had drunk a little and smoked much. She smiled to herself, as though she were happy. Very carefully she set about touching up her cheeks and her lips, and then walked casually out into the street.

PENGUIN MODERN CLASSICS

THE PLAGUE
ALBERT CAMUS

'Camus's great novel rings truer than ever; a fireball in the night of complacency'
Tony Judt

The townspeople of Oran are in the grip of a deadly plague, which condemns its victims to a swift and horrifying death. Fear, isolation and claustrophobia follow as they are forced into quarantine, each responding in their own way to the lethal bacillus: some resign themselves to fate, some seek blame and a few, like Dr Rieux, resist the terror.

An immediate triumph when it was published in 1947, Camus' novel is in part an allegory for France's suffering under the Nazi occupation, and also a story of bravery and determination against the precariousness of human existence.

'An impressive new translation ... of this matchless fable of fear, courage and cowardice' *Independent*

Translated by Robin Buss
With an Introduction by Tony Judt

WINNER OF THE NOBEL PRIZE FOR LITERATURE

PENGUIN MODERN CLASSICS

THE AGE OF REASON
JEAN-PAUL SARTRE

'For my money ... the greatest novel of the post-war period' Philip Kerr

Set in the volatile Paris summer of 1938, *The Age of Reason* follows two days in the life of Mathieu Delarue, a philosophy teacher, and his circle in the cafés and bars of Montparnasse. Mathieu Delarue has so far managed to contain sex and personal freedom in conveniently separate compartments. But now he is in trouble, urgently trying to raise 4,000 francs to procure a safe abortion for his mistress, Marcelle. Beyond all this, filtering an uneasy light on his predicament, rises the distant thread of the coming of the Second World War.

The Age of Reason is the first volume in Sartre's *Roads to Freedom* trilogy.

Translated by Eric Sutton
With an Introduction by David Caute

PENGUIN MODERN CLASSICS

LITTLE BIRDS
ANAÏS NIN

'One of the most extraordinary and unconventional writers of this century' *The New York Times Book Review*

Delta of Venus and *Little Birds*, Anaïs Nin's bestselling volumes of erotica, contain striking revelations of a woman's sexuality and inner life. In *Little Birds*, each of the thirteen short stories captures a moment of sexual awakening, recognition or fulfilment, and reveals the subtle or explicit means by which men and women are aroused. Lust, obsession, fantasy and desire emerge as part of the human condition, as pure or as complex as any other of its aspects.

Delta of Venus is also published by Penguin Classics.

PENGUIN MODERN CLASSICS

BLUE OF NOON
GEORGES BATAILLE

Set against the backdrop of Europe's slide into Fascism, *Blue of Noon* is a blackly compelling account of depravity and violence. As its narrator lurches despairingly from city to city in a surreal sexual and mental nightmare of squalor, sadism and drunken encounters, his internal collapse mirrors the fighting and marching on the streets outside. Exploring the dark forces beneath the surface of civilization, this is a novel torn between identifying with history's victims and being seduced by the monstrous glamour of its terrible victors, and is one of the twentieth century's great nihilist works.

'There's a kind of exhilaration in this – and a kind of terror' Will Self

Penguin Modern Classics

WIDE SARGASSO SEA
JEAN RHYS

'Rhys took one of the works of genius of the nineteenth century and turned it inside-out to create one of the works of genius of the twentieth century'
Michèle Roberts, *The Times*

Jean Rhys's late literary masterpiece, *Wide Sargasso Sea*, was inspired by Charlotte Brontë's *Jane Eyre*, and is set in the lush, beguiling landscape of Jamaica in the 1830s.

Born into an oppressive colonialist society, Creole heiress Antoinette Cosway meets a young Englishman who is drawn to her innocent sensuality and beauty. After their marriage, disturbing rumours begin to circulate, poisoning her husband against her. Caught between his demands and her own precarious sense of belonging, Antoinette is driven towards madness.

PENGUIN MODERN CLASSICS

THE IMMORALIST
ANDRÉ GIDE

'Few writers in the twentieth century have been as influential as André Gide'
Contemporary Review

Michel knows nothing about love when he marries the gentle Marceline out of duty
to his father. They travel to Tunisia for their honeymoon, where Michel becomes
very ill. During his recovery, he meets a young Arab boy, whose radiant health and
beauty captivate him. This is an awakening for him both sexually and morally and,
in seeking to live according to his own desires, Michel discovers a new freedom.
But, as he also finds, freedom can be a burden.

'*L'Immoraliste* confronts "the fundamental, eternal problem of the moral
conditions of our existence", the gap between what we were and what we have
become' Alan Sheridan

Translated by David Watson
With an Introduction by Alan Sheridan

read more ⓟ

PENGUIN MODERN CLASSICS

GIOVANNI'S ROOM
JAMES BALDWIN

'Exquisite … a feat of fire-breathing, imaginative daring' *Guardian*

David, a young American in 1950s Paris, is waiting for his fiancée to return from vacation in Spain. But when he meets Giovanni, a handsome Italian barman, the two men are drawn into an intense affair. After three months David's fiancée returns, and, denying his true nature, David rejects Giovanni for a 'safe' future as a married man. His decision eventually brings tragedy.

Full of passion, regret and longing, this story of a fated love triangle has become a landmark in gay writing, but its appeal is broader. James Baldwin caused outrage as a black author writing about white homosexuals, yet for him the issues of race, sexuality and personal freedom were eternally intertwined.

'Audacious … remarkable … elegant and courageous' Caryl Phillips

With a new Introduction by Caryl Phillips

Penguin Modern Classics

TO THE LIGHTHOUSE
VIRGINIA WOOLF

To the Lighthouse is at once a vivid impressionist depiction of a family holiday, and a meditation on a marriage, on parenthood and childhood, on grief, tyranny and bitterness. Its use of stream of consciousness, reminiscence and shifting perspectives gives the novel an intimate, poetic essence, and at the time of publication in 1927 it represented an utter rejection of Victorian and Edwardian literary values.

Virginia Woolf saw the novel as an elegy to her own parents, and in her diary she wrote: 'I used to think of him [father] and mother daily: but writing *The Lighthouse* laid them in my mind.'

Edited by Stella McNichol

With an Introduction and Notes by Hermione Lee

PENGUIN MODERN CLASSICS

THE MAGICIAN OF LUBLIN
ISAAC BASHEVIS SINGER

Yasha the magician – sword swallower, fire eater, acrobat and master of escape – is famed for his extraordinary Houdini-like skills. Half Jewish, half Gentile, a free thinker who slips easily between worlds, Yasha has an observant wife, a loyal assistant who travels with him and a woman in every town. Now, though, his exploits are catching up with him, and he is tempted to make one final escape – from his marriage, his homeland and the last tendrils of his father's religion. Set in Warsaw and the shtetls of the 1870s, Isaac Bashevis Singer's second novel is a haunting psychological portrait of a man's flight from love.

Winner of the Nobel Prize for Literature

'A spellbinder as clever as Scheherazade; he arrests the reader at once, transports him to a far place and a far, improbable time and does not let him go until the end'
New Republic

'Singer writes with a love and passion unequalled in contemporary fiction'
Washington Post

Penguin Modern Classics

THE FLOOD
J.M.G. LE CLÉZIO

François Besson listens to a tape recording of a girl contemplating suicide. Drifting through the days in a provincial city, he thoughtlessly starts a fire in his apartment, attends confession, and examines, with great intentness but without affection, a naked woman he wakes beside. And, as Besson moves through an ugly and threatening rain, his thoughts eventually lead to violence, first turned outward and then directed languidly against himself.

'This terrifying vision of existence is conveyed with intense poetic power'
Guardian

'His distinctive talent is everywhere evident, so that in Peter Green's admirable translation many individual scenes have a horrific hallucinatory power'
Sunday Times

Penguin Modern Classics

A HEART SO WHITE
JAVIER MARÍAS

'The most subtle and gifted writer in contemporary Spanish literature' *Boston Globe*

In the middle of a family lunch Teresa, just married, goes to the bathroom, unbuttons her blouse and shoots herself in the heart. What made her kill herself immediately after her honeymoon? Years later, this mystery fascinates the young newlywed Juan, whose father was married to Teresa before he married Juan's mother. As Juan edges closer to the truth, he begins to question his own relationships, and whether he really wants to know what happened. Haunting and unsettling, *A Heart So White* is a breathtaking portrayal of two generations, two marriages, the relentless power of the past and the terrible price of knowledge.

With a new Introduction by Jonathan Coe

'The work of a supreme stylist ... It is brilliantly done' James Woodall, *The Times*